April 2010

To: Rebecca

Tunnels
of TIME

A MOOSE JAW ADVENTURE

Follow Your Heart!

TUNNELS
of TIME

A MOOSE JAW ADVENTURE

MARY HARELKIN BISHOP

COTEAU BOOKS
TWENTY-FIVE YEARS

This novel is a work of fiction. Names, characters, places, and incidents either are the product of the author's imagination or are used fictitiously. Any resemblance to actual persons, living or dead, is coincidental.

Edited by Barbara Sapergia
Cover image and interior illustration by Dawn Pearcey
Cover and book design by Duncan Campbell
Printed and bound in Canada at Transcontinental Printing

National Library of Canada Cataloguing in Publication Data

Bishop, Mary Harelkin, 1958-
Tunnels of time
ISBN 1-55050-164-X

I. Title.

PS8553.I849T85 2000   jC813'.6   C00-920038-X
PZ7.B5264Tu 2000

ELEVENTH PRINTING

2517 Victoria Avenue
Regina, Saskatchewan
Canada   S4P 0T2

Available in Canada from:
Publishers Group Canada
9050 Shaughnessy Street
Vancouver, BC V6P 6E5

The publisher gratefully acknowledges the financial assistance of the Saskatchewan Arts Board, the Canada Council for the Arts, the Government of Canada through the Book Publishing Industry Development Program (BPIDP), and the City of Regina Arts Commission, for its publishing program.

TABLE *of* CONTENTS

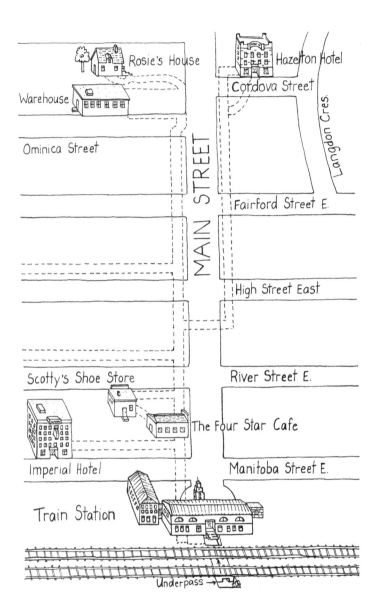

ABOVE GROUND

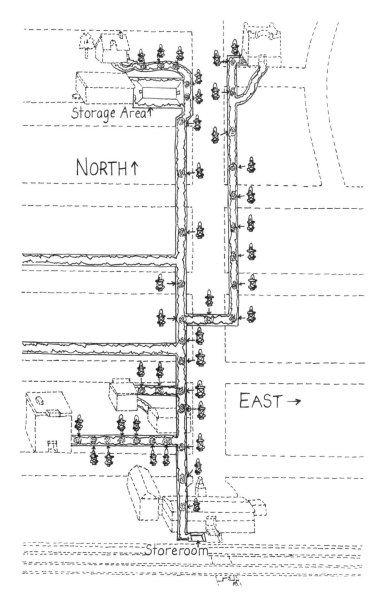

Storage Area↑

NORTH↑

EAST →

Storeroom

THE TUNNELS BELOW

to Garth, Ryan, and Nerissa

5:15 PM Friday Evening

NOT MOOSE JAW!

"Just be civilized, Andrea," Mrs. Talbot pleaded. "That's all I ask. It's only for the weekend. It's not a life sentence."

"It feels that way to me." Andrea folded her arms and sank further down in the back seat of the family's old sedan. "I don't even like Vanessa!"

"Yes," her mother sighed. "You've certainly made that point well known over the years."

Andrea turned her head to the window, hoping that her parents would finally leave her alone. They had been lecturing her for the whole trip and it was getting to be more than she could handle.

The speed of the car ate up the final few prairie

1

miles and she watched unseeing as farmers' fields whizzed by, drawing her ever closer to Moose Jaw, a small city situated in the southern half of Saskatchewan.

"It'll be fun, Andy!" Tony fairly bubbled over with enthusiasm. His eight-year-old zest for life was almost contagious; almost, but not quite. He sat in the back seat on the opposite side of the car, bouncing up and down with excitement. "All that good food and lots of cousins to play with. And Crazy Aunt Bea." Tony giggled gleefully as he playfully nudged Andrea in the ribs. He knew that Aunt Bea had a special fondness for Andrea that nearly drove her batty.

Great Aunt Bea, Grandpa Talbot's younger sister, just wasn't normal, at least not in Andrea's mind. She was a big woman who wore the most flamboyant, outlandish clothes Andrea had ever seen. Everything about Aunt Bea called attention to her. Her gaudy dangling earrings swung precariously from her stretched earlobes every time she moved her head. And she gestured dramatically when she spoke, which was always in a loud baritone voice that seemed to carry for miles, especially, it seemed, when she was trying to whisper.

"It'll be fun for you, squirt," Andrea retorted, brown eyes blazing. "But I'm missing the most awesome mountain bike trip of all time! And for what?" she wailed. "To be a stupid junior bridesmaid in some stupid wedding party."

"Right now," she checked the Mickey Mouse watch on her wrist, "I should be on the bus with forty other mountain bikers heading to Banff. Instead, I'm going to be stuck in dumb old Moose Jaw with dizzy cousin Vanessa and her blasted wedding."

"There will be other bike trips." Mr. Talbot spoke slowly and deliberately from the front passenger seat. He appeared to be watching the scenery fly by, but Andrea knew from past experience that all of his attention was pinned on her. His patience was wearing thin; she could hear the steel edge of his usually even-tempered, quiet voice. Her mother was a more relaxed driver than her dad. Mrs. Talbot did almost all of the driving, both in the city and on long highway trips.

Mr. Talbot sighed and rubbed his eyes. "I am truly sorry that both your cousin's wedding and the bike trip fell on the July long weekend, but that's life. These kinds of things happen all the time. We may not like it, but we have to deal with it as best we can." He paused, turning halfway in his seat to regard Andrea, who sat directly behind him.

Andrea met his gaze and shrugged her shoulders in defeat. "I know, Dad," she said quietly. "I'll get a grip and deal with it." He smiled his thanks and turned around again. "This is called 'character building,' right Dad?"

Mr. Talbot smiled over his shoulder. "You are

3

growing up, Andy," he said, "even if you don't feel like you are. After all, you are thirteen."

"Thanks, honey." Mrs. Talbot smiled into the rear-view mirror at Andrea. "I knew we could count on you."

"I don't want to be a junior bridesmaid at Vanessa's wedding. Oh, Mom, what happens if I do something really stupid like – like drop the flowers? What if I trip into the other bridesmaids and we all fall into a huge heap? I'd be so embarrassed and everyone would know it was all my fault," Andrea moaned, her worst fears growing more immense as she voiced her concerns.

"Yeah," Tony rubbed his hands gleefully. "And it would probably all be on video. Everyone videotapes big events these days. We could call it 'Andrea's Worst Wedding Nightmare' and sell it for millions. I bet we could sell it to that funny video show on TV!"

"Tony." Mr. Talbot spoke sternly from the front seat. "That's enough. Andrea, honey, nothing like that will happen. You'll do fine, you'll see."

"I don't know why Vanessa wanted you to be a junior bridesmaid, anyway," Tony piped up. "You always treat her so mean." Andrea halfheartedly elbowed him in the ribs as she settled back into the seat, her worries eating away at her.

The edge of the city came into sight. Car lots, restaurants, and hotels lined the Main Street of Moose

Jaw. Signs warned that the speed limits were reduced ahead and Mrs. Talbot dutifully released the cruise control, allowing the car to gradually slow down to fifty kilometres per hour for city driving.

It was true though, Andrea realized. She had pulled some mean and terrible pranks on her older cousin Vanessa. Maybe it was because Vanessa was eight years older and so much prettier, with her dark naturally curly hair and sparkling blue eyes. Perhaps it was because Vanessa was so gullible and naive. That made pulling pranks on her very easy. It might even have been because Vanessa was so intelligent in other ways. Whatever the reason, Andrea had pulled classic pranks on Vanessa over the years and, as she had grown and matured in the past few months, she had begun to feel guilty about the terrible and sometimes hurtful things she had done to Vanessa.

"Remember the time you cut off one of her pigtails in the middle of the night?" Tony recalled. Andrea elbowed him again, harder this time.

"Shhh," she warned. "I've never been forgiven for that particular stunt."

"As I recall," Mrs. Talbot interrupted, having over-heard Tony's remark, "that was your last stunt." She smiled menacingly over the back seat at Andrea. "I wonder why."

Andrea grimaced as she remembered the trouble she had gotten into over that prank. Everyone was horrified, especially poor Vanessa, who had almost passed out in shock. Andrea had had a hard time explaining her actions that time. They wanted nothing but the truth, and it was the one thing Andrea could not admit. She could barely admit to herself that she was jealous of Vanessa's dark flowing curls and pretty blue eyes. Her own hair was blonde thin straw, which she kept cropped so short she was often mistaken for a boy. Sometimes, Andrea thought ruefully, the only way to tell the difference was that she usually wore barrettes, as she was doing today.

"Look," Andrea pointed, trying to change the subject. "Here's the long hill where Tony almost killed himself learning to roller blade." The long hill was part of Main Street and led down into the centre of the city. "How many stitches did it take?" she asked, even though she knew the answer. It was one way to get everyone's mind off herself and Vanessa and onto something else.

"Twenty-seven," Tony declared proudly, although he hadn't been quite as brave at the time. He had been in excruciating pain. Tony watched the houses and buildings stream by as the car travelled down the hill. "Boy, I'll never try that again!"

Main Street was busy this Friday evening and finding a parking spot was proving difficult. "There's the restaurant." Mrs. Talbot pointed to a well-lit place at the end of Main Street.

"And there's my favourite building in all of Moose Jaw." Mr. Talbot pointed across Manitoba Street to a huge old building. "I see that developers have put a new store in that old railway station. It looks open for business. It's a grand old building, I'm glad they've put it to good use again."

"I'll drop you off here in front of the restaurant and go find a place to park," Mrs. Talbot interrupted. She stopped and double-parked while everyone quickly scrambled out of the car. "Be nice," she warned Andrea as she shut the car door, "especially to Aunt Bea. She seems to be easily upset these days." Andrea nodded reluctantly. There wasn't much else she could be, not with them watching her like hawks all weekend. As for Aunt Bea, Andrea had learned to ignore her, tolerate her even, though she wished Aunt Bea didn't cling to her so. It was embarrassing at times. Andrea pushed the car door shut firmly and turned to join the others on the sidewalk.

Mr. Talbot was staring open-mouthed. "Is that what you wore to a wedding rehearsal?" he asked, clearly shocked at her choice of clothing. "Oh, I should have checked to see what you had on when we left!"

"Dad, you kept me busy cleaning out the garage until the last second, remember? You wanted the job done before we left. And anyway, you didn't tell me I needed to dress up."

"I am Vanessa's godfather. And you're old enough to know what to wear for a special occasion. I expected you to wear something decent!" He looked down his nose at Andrea's attire.

"What's wrong with what I'm wearing?" Andrea asked, belligerently looking down at her tattered old bib overalls and ancient, misshapen greyish T-shirt. In a fit of rebellion at having to miss the bike trip, she had unearthed the offending clothes from the bottom of her closet only this morning. She had deliberately worn the outfit to get even with someone, and now she wasn't sure who that someone was. Oh well, Andrea sighed to herself, what was done was done. She couldn't change now – everything else she owned was either at home, safe in her closet, or stuffed into her suitcase in the car.

"Oh, never mind," her father sighed wearily. "At least you're here and not sulking anymore."

It was on the tip of Andrea's tongue; a rude retort about the fact that she never sulked. But she stopped herself just in time and let the moment pass. A war of words with her father would be a great stress reliever for her, but probably not for her father. She shut her mouth and resolutely followed her brother into the quaint restaurant, The Four Star Café.

The wedding party had reserved the banquet room for dinner that night. The restaurant was a landmark – a heritage building that had been built when Moose

Jaw was growing and thriving in the early 1900s. It had been refurbished over the years. With its high ceilings of embossed tin and its high-backed wooden benches, it made Andrea feel as if she had stepped back in time. The atmosphere was really rather pleasing and she wondered why her own family had never eaten here before on other trips to Moose Jaw.

The rehearsal was to take place after supper, which was unusual. Most often, wedding rehearsals came first, followed by a meal. But because part of the Talbot family, namely Andrea's branch of the family tree, had had to travel a long way and would be hungry after the long trip, it was decided to do it the other way around.

Mr. Saunders, the owner, escorted them to the narrow, steep stairs at the back of the restaurant. They led down to the banquet room. Andrea could hear music and laughter as they descended. She firmly put the bike trip out of her mind and pasted a smile on her face. Moose Jaw would be boring, she knew. Nothing could compare to the excitement and exhilaration of biking in the mountains – but she was stuck here for the long weekend and knew that she had better make the best of it. She envied her friends, though. Boy, would they ever have a lot to tell her when they got back.

There were greetings and hugs galore as cousins, sisters, uncles, grandparents, and friends were reunited. Andrea was drawn into the midst of it, the bike trip temporarily forgotten. Everyone had a comment about her, either on her choice of dress – Aunt Frieda said: "Doesn't your mother know how to dress you?" – or about her being the junior bridesmaid – Cousin Tom declared: "A little too clumsy, aren't you, Octopus Andy? You'll end up tripping on your dress and falling off your high heels. And with that short haircut, you hardly even look like a girl."

Andrea felt her insides grow cold. Cousin Tom had just voiced her worst fears. Even he seemed to know that she wouldn't do a good job. Why hadn't Vanessa chosen someone else?

At thirteen Andrea felt pretty mature, but she was very small for her age. She looked more like a ten-year-old boy than a thirteen-year-old girl, and she was just as flat chested, much to her dismay. It didn't help matters that her two best friends had started to develop in Grade Six and were now fully blossomed in the bosom department.

"My princess, a junior bridesmaid," Grandma Talbot cooed in Andrea's ear as she planted a loud, smacking kiss on her cheek. "Imagine that."

Tony sidled up to Andrea and whispered at her elbow, "Here comes Aunt Bea. She'll be flapping all over you in a minute, buzz-buzz!" He moved his arms minutely so that his parents wouldn't see, mimicking Aunt Bea's approach.

Andrea swatted at Tony's arms and he jumped away. "She's really not that bad," Andrea defended, "just – different, that's all."

Aunt Bea swooped down on Andrea like a giant bumblebee to nectar, enveloping her in a big hug. "Andrea Talbot, darling!" she fairly screamed. Her pure white hair was piled high on her head. Thick glasses balanced on her nose, allowing striking blue eyes to peek over the top of the frames.

Andrea found herself engulfed in clouds of brightly coloured material. "Hello, Aunt Bea," she greeted, allowing herself to be hugged. She glanced up into Aunt Bea's beaming face. For a woman in her eighties, her skin was very clear, with few wrinkles. Her eyes crinkled and sparkled back at Andrea. Why, she must have been beautiful as a young woman, Andrea suddenly thought. She limply returned the hug as Tony made gagging noises behind Bea's back.

Aunt Bea might be over eighty, but she was agile. As she released Andrea, she whirled around, long thin arms snaking out to catch Tony by surprise. She pulled him into a bear hug, laughing merrily. "I've got eyes in the back of my head. You might remember that the next time you try making faces at me behind my back." Tony wriggled out of her grasp, but not before Aunt Bea had planted a noisy red kiss on his cheek.

"Anything new and exciting happen lately, Andrea Talbot?" Bea suddenly inquired, turning her attention back to Andrea. She watched Andrea's face anxiously, as if looking for something.

She is a strange old bird, Andrea thought, not for the first time. Why does she always ask me the same question, in just that tone? "Nothing's new, Aunt Bea," she replied in a resigned voice. Except that I'm missing the most awesome bike trip of all time. She closed her mouth tightly to capture and hold those potent words from escaping her lips. Perhaps she really was growing up.

Tony tugged on Aunt Bea's pale, thin arm. "Why do you always call Andrea, 'Andrea Talbot'?" he demanded. "Almost all of us are Talbots here."

"Oh-h-h, well-ll," Aunt Bea was suddenly flustered. She flapped her arms and wrung her hands until she looked like a giant insect trying to take off. "There's no reason, really," Aunt Bea sputtered. "I-I just like the sound of it – Andrea Talbot." She pronounced the name slowly, savouring the feel of it on her tongue. "It has a nice ring to it."

"Well, I think it's dumb," Tony declared with childlike logic and Andrea had to agree. It was an eccentric thing to do. She could not remember a time that Aunt Bea had ever called her just Andrea or even Andy; it was always Andrea Talbot. As if Andrea would forget her own last name or something.

Once, when Andrea was Tony's age, she had been assertive, asking Aunt Bea to please quit calling her

Andrea Talbot. "Just call me, Andy," Andrea had begged. This had been during her real tomboy years when she had insisted on being Andy.

"Oh-h-h," Aunt Bea had replied, obviously quite upset by the idea. "I could never do that. It would bring back too many memories."

"Memories?" the young Andy had repeated.

Aunt Bea had patted her on the head. "Yes, darling. Memories. Someday, you may understand, Andrea Talbot...or perhaps you never will.... It's hard to say...." Aunt Bea had flapped away to join the older generation of Talbots that day, leaving Andy with many unanswered questions bouncing around in her head. The questions still hadn't been answered and Aunt Bea was still calling Andrea by her two names. Some things never changed, Andrea thought with a sigh. She shook her head to clear it of her daydreams, just in time to see Cousin Richard appear at her side.

"Vanessa sure got the last joke on you," pesky Richard declared. He had snuck up from behind Andrea and punched her arm, a little too hard to be playful. The damage done, he then moved on to arm wrestle with Tony over in the corner near an ancient looking piece of furniture.

"Be careful of that armoire, boys," Andrea's mother warned. She had the awesome ability of being able to monitor everyone's actions at once.

"She has eyes in the back of her head too," Tony

groaned, "just like Aunt Bea."

Grandpa Talbot spotted Andrea and hurried over, wrapping her in a huge bear hug. "How's my girl?" he asked, his blue eyes twinkling brightly against leathery tan skin and crisp white hair. It was amazing how much he and Aunt Bea looked alike. They could have passed for twins, even though Grandpa was a few years old than his sister.

Andrea sank into her grandfather's embrace, allowing herself to be engulfed. She pressed her nose against his best black suit jacket and sniffed – peppermint, as always. Some things never changed, such as the scent of her grandfather's clothes. "Oh Grandpa," Andrea sighed, "I really don't want to be here." The words slipped out before she could catch them and she felt guilty again. She didn't want to hurt her grandfather's feelings.

"I know, honey." Grandpa hugged her closer. "Sometimes we have to let family come first. That's the way it is."

"I guess...." Andrea drew a little away from his warm embrace to look up into his kind eyes. "It isn't that I don't love my family – well, most of them...." She glanced from Aunt Bea, who was busy talking to Grandma Talbot, to Vanessa and back again, guiltily.

Grandpa cleared his throat noisily, a sign that he was nervous and wanted to say something important. "About Bea, Andrea –"

"It's okay, Grandpa," Andrea interrupted. "I really don't mind Aunt Bea, it's just that sometimes she seems too – too –"

"Intense," Grandpa Talbot supplied when Andrea was silent, searching for the right word.

"Yes, exactly. And I don't understand it. I don't understand her either. She scares me sometimes, Grandpa," Andrea admitted. "It's almost as if she knows some secrets about me that I don't even know myself. But how could that be?" Andrea didn't worry about discussing such things with her grandfather. She knew that she could always be honest with him. For some unexplained reason, he too had taken a special shine to Andrea when she was just a baby. That bond was still strong.

Grandpa patted Andrea's shoulder consolingly. "You don't need to be afraid of her, Andrea. She would never do anything to hurt you. In fact, quite the opposite. Maybe some day, you'll understand." He was quiet for a moment, letting the thought sink in. "Perhaps Bea is, in a way, trying to live life through you. It happens sometimes...." Grandfather seemed to be talking more to himself than to Andrea. He had a faraway look in his eyes as he stared off over Andrea's head in the direction of the armoire situated in the corner of the restaurant.

"Grandpa?" Andrea questioned, alarm causing her voice to rise. "Are you all right?"

Grandfather quickly roused himself, shaking his

head ruefully. "Just daydreaming, dear." He chuckled loudly, then cleared his throat noisily again and abruptly changed the subject. "You can't choose your relatives, Andrea. You're stuck with us. Speaking of which, here comes Vanessa now." Grandfather quickly caught Vanessa's eye across the noisy crowded room and gestured with his head, smiling and pointing down at Andrea.

Why, he *is* changing the subject, Andrea thought in amazement. There was a mystery here, she was sure of it. And somehow it involved her. Andrea couldn't think of anything mysterious that had happened to her in her young life, but she would find out. Supersleuth Andrea loved a good mystery and this one was particularly interesting, since it seemed to be all about her and her weird but wonderful family.

Tucking all thoughts of the mystery away, Andrea watched covertly as Vanessa approached her from across the room, towing a handsome man along by the hand. That must be Greg, Andrea guessed, Vanessa's fiancé. She searched Vanessa's face carefully for signs of contempt or superiority, but found only the glow of anticipation and joy. "Thank you for being my junior bridesmaid," Vanessa said with sincerity when she reached Andrea's side. "There is no one else I'd rather have than you." Andrea pressed her lips into a smile and gave Vanessa a weak hug. Her feelings toward Vanessa were suddenly ambiguous, sliding between guilt and envy at any given moment. "I want you to meet Greg." Vanessa smiled happily, pulling Greg into the conversation. She leaned against him and gazed up into his boyish face. "Greg, this is Andrea."

Greg stuck out a huge paw, engulfing Andrea's dainty hand in his. "Nice to meet you, Andrea. I've heard a lot about you." He smiled brightly at Andrea and the hair on the back of her neck stood up in alarm. She could just tell that he knew something embarrassing, and she was right. "I've wanted to meet you for ages, ever since I heard about the haircutting episode." He laughed loudly while Andrea felt heat rise up into her face. She wished the floor would open up and swallow her whole.

"Greg," Vanessa scolded lightly. "Don't embarrass Andrea like that. That happened a long time ago, and I'm sure Andrea would rather forget about it. Go and talk to Grandpa now so Andrea and I can have a little chat."

"Sorry," Greg grinned. He didn't look one bit apologetic to Andrea. She watched uncomfortably while Greg leaned over to peck Vanessa's cheek. "Be careful, honey. You'd better check for scissors before you get too close," he teased, as he turned away in search of Grandfather Talbot. Vanessa swatted playfully at his retreating back.

"Sorry about that, Andrea. And don't worry about Greg, he's just a big tease. Tom told him all about the hair incident. I'd almost forgotten about it." Andrea nodded mutely, searching wildly for something to say as an awkward silence stretched between the girls.

"Gee, I love your barrettes," Vanessa suddenly exclaimed. She reached to touch the two barrettes holding Andrea's hair back from her face, one on each side of her head. "Where did you get them?"

"I-I made them," Andrea reluctantly admitted. She suddenly felt very young and naive. Only a five year old would wear juvenile barrettes like that. They were nothing special; just ordinary white plastic onto which Andrea had glued letters to spell out her name: "Andrea" on the left barrette and "Talbot" on the right.

"Would you make me a pair, Andrea?" Vanessa asked shyly.

"Really?!" Andrea gushed, suddenly pleased that she had worn the barrettes and that Vanessa liked them.

"Of course," Vanessa replied honestly. She patted her beautiful curly locks. "I need something to help keep this mop out of my eyes. And the barrettes are awfully cute."

At that moment Andrea thought Vanessa must be the best cousin in the world. She impulsively threw her arms around her. "I'll make them for you as soon as I get back home," she promised. It seemed that Vanessa had finally forgiven her for cutting her hair.

Grandpa took his pocket watch out of his pants

pocket. It had a large gold-faced lid covering the face of the watch, which always kept toddlers enthralled for hours. The lid snapped open with the push of a button to reveal the time on a rather simple face. Two elegant black hands pointed to the correct numbers. It was an ancient watch, probably older than Grandpa, and Andrea loved it.

Grandpa checked the time on his beloved watch and made an announcement, "We need to get a move on things if we're going to stay on schedule," he warned his chattering family. He neatly snapped the lid on his watch and slid it deftly back into his pants pocket.

The relatives began to move. Soon they were all seated around a long banquet table and news and gossip spread back and forth with a speed that would have put the first telegraph operators out of business. Orders were being taken by a young waitress, with old Mr. Saunders overseeing the large group. He was outdoing himself with overt cheerfulness and service, wiping at a damp spot here, rearranging a place setting there. Probably hoping that they would spend a lot of money, Andrea thought cynically. She noticed, as he stopped to chat briefly with her grandparents, that he had a faint scar running the length of one cheek. How strange, Andrea thought, trying not to stare. She studied him from under her eyelashes, comparing him to her grandfather. Mr. Saunders appeared to be slightly younger, with thinning grey hair and piercing eyes. She figured that he was probably in his seventies, though it was difficult to tell.

Drinks were served and the large party visited loudly and boisterously as they waited for supper, exchanging jokes and telling stories. The restaurant owner got into the act too. "Have you heard of the Moose Jaw tunnels?" he asked, as he served Andrea and her parents their beverages.

"Tunnels?" Tony piped up, his eyes aglow with excitement.

"I've heard a bit," Mrs. Talbot commented, "but I'm sure we're all interested in learning more." She nodded encouragingly at her immediate family as if to say, "Be nice, or else."

Like an exuberant tour guide, old Mr. Saunders gave his spiel: "Businesses along Main Street and a few other places have discovered underground tunnels linking one building to another."

"What were the tunnels used for?" Tony wanted to know. "And who built them?"

"We only have theories right now," Mr. Saunders answered, his eyes snapping with excitement. Anyone could tell that he loved history and particularly enjoyed telling the story of the Moose Jaw tunnels. His greying hair bounced on his head as he cleared his throat, and Andrea decided, unkindly, that he was probably old enough to have lived the stories he was about to tell.

"One theory is that the Chinese immigrants who

came in with the railway companies to build the railways built the tunnels as places to hide when their other work was finished in Canada. They wanted to stay in Canada, but didn't have the 'Head Tax,' as it was called, to pay for their citizenship. Another theory is that the tunnels were used by the gangsters of the 1920s during Prohibition to hide gamblers and illegal liquor from the police." He chuckled to himself.

"Quiet old Moose Jaw was really a swinging town back then. It had quite a wild reputation. In fact, one of its nicknames was 'Little Chicago,' since rumour has it that gangsters did business here."

"Wow!" Tony breathed. "That's cool. I wanna see a tunnel. But, what's pro-prohab —"

"Prohibition," Mr. Saunders supplied, "was the period of time when alcohol was illegal in many of the states in the United States. Rumour has it that gangsters such as Al Capone travelled on the Soo Line Railway up to Moose Jaw to get liquor and to avoid the police. Supposedly, they used the tunnels to move from place to place unnoticed."

"Neat!" Tony enthused. "Now can I see a tunnel?"

"Yes, you sure can," Mr. Saunders asserted. "Just follow me."

"Follow you where?" Tony asked warily. He was a little reluctant to leave the warm, bright safety of the restaurant.

Mr. Saunders laughed. "Just over to the wall," he

said, pointing to the large armoire standing in the corner. "We have two tunnels right here in this restaurant."

"Wow!" Tony repeated, jumping from his chair. "Let me see." Andrea's parents seemed anxious to see the tunnels too and rushed after Tony.

Mr. Saunders had pointed first to the corner of the basement closest to Main Street, then at one of the back corners. Andrea stared at the corners, but saw nothing. The tunnels were obviously well camouflaged, not visible unless directly pointed out.

Her parents and Tony headed for the Main Street tunnel. Andrea reluctantly tagged along, curious, but not wanting to appear overeager. Tunnels? In Moose Jaw? It must be some kind of tourist gimmick, she decided. Just a reason to get ordinary travellers to stop in small-town Saskatchewan and spend a few hard-earned dollars.

Tony went in first. "Don't tell them what you see," the owner warned mischievously. "Let them see it for themselves."

"I won't," Tony promised. He walked in and out rather quickly, a "Wow!" of appreciation forming on his lips. "Where's the other one?" he asked eagerly. He looked around the restaurant, carefully studying the walls. The first tunnel was fairly visible, if you knew what you were looking for and if you knew where to look, Andrea thought. The second one was more difficult to find and Tony's searching eyes discerned nothing unusual. He set off in search of the second tunnel, which Mr. Saunders indicated was just behind the huge armoire on the other side of the basement.

While Tony pushed the armoire away from the corner, Andrea waited impatiently for her turn at the first tunnel, digging the toe of her dirty runner into the thick grey carpet of the restaurant floor. She noticed with scorn that the carpet wound its way around the corner. It appeared to go right into the tunnel. What kind of joke was this anyway? No authentic tunnel would have carpet in it.

Andrea was last, behind both parents, and watched uncomfortably as each person went into the tunnel, oohed and ahed over the mystery, and came back out with a conspiratorial smile. She wasn't impressed with this game. What could they be seeing that caused such delight on their faces? It seemed silly and nonsensical. "Are you sure you didn't build these tunnels as a publicity stunt for your restaurant?" Andrea rudely asked Mr. Saunders over her shoulder as she rushed into the tunnel.

Her intention was to rush right back out again, cool and nonchalant, but things didn't quite work out that way. Andrea was in such a hurry that she didn't hear, or perhaps just didn't heed, Mr. Saunders's warning to slow down. She rounded the corner of the entrance to the tunnel at a fast pace and crashed directly into what looked to be…her own reflection! It was a mirror!

That was Andrea's last thought as lights began to flash before her eyes. Waves of sound seemed to pound her body, fluorescent beams of bright light washed over her. Legs suddenly weak, Andrea sank to the floor. She felt the sensation of movement, as if she were travelling at high speeds through vacuous space. Andrea heard running feet and voices calling her name from afar. It was dark, so black that she couldn't see her hand reach up to rub her pounding head. The ground felt cool and damp, even in her thick overalls. Andrea tried to get up, but found herself frozen to the ground. She put her hands on the floor to push herself into a sitting position. Gravel moved under her body. Where was the carpet, she wondered. She should be lying on the warm thick carpet of the restaurant, not this cold, damp earth.

Suddenly something was pulling her arm, drawing her further into the tunnel. "Let go of me!" Andrea called out, trying to free her arm. The thing on the other end had a strong grip and pulled her more fully into the tunnel, dragging her every inch of the way.

6:30 PM Friday Evening

WHERE AM I?

The first thing Andrea noticed was that it was dark – too dark to see exactly what was in front of her. It was also very damp and cramped. She felt as if she was in a tight, narrow space, and her arm was still being pulled, propelling her trembling body further and further into the dark, damp tunnel. Whoever or whatever had her arm was strong. It had pulled her from a semi-lying position to her shaky feet with very little effort.

"Stop!" Andrea yelled as she gave a mighty jerk of her arm and almost pulled herself free. The thing in front of her turned to face her. In the eerie light cast by a lantern hanging near by, Andrea could just make out a shape. It was a boy about her age. He was dressed much like her, in dungarees, a plaid shirt, and dark blue cap, but he looked different somehow; not like the average, ordinary teenager of the times. His clothes were too old looking, and his hair was a very weird style. It hung around the tips of his ears in a roughly rounded shape, as if a little kid had hacked at it with dull scissors. "Who are you?" Andrea demanded, frightened at the darkness and the strangeness of the boy. "And where am I?"

"Look, mate!" the young voice declared. "I was told to meet ya in the tunnel and show ya the ropes tonight. Yer late – I thought you musta chickened out. If you're a namby-pamby and afraid of the dark, then this ain't the job for you, see?"

"J-job?" Andrea stuttered. She was utterly and totally confused.

"Ya know, workin' the tunnels."

"T-tunnels?" She stuttered, staring at the youth.

"Ya stupid, are ya? How come I always end up with the guys with no smarts!" Andrea could dimly make out his gesture as he tapped his head with his finger and made little circles in the air around his right ear.

"Look, do ya want the job or not? I ain't got all day to wait for ya. I got work to do. There's rumours Ol' Scarface is in town tonight and that usually means lots of business and excitement."

"I don't want a job," Andrea declared, brushing

herself off and checking for more sore spots. "Just point me back to that restaurant I was just at and I'll go back to my wedding rehearsal."

"Sure thing, pal." The boy obligingly turned and pointed down the pitch black tunnel. "It's back there a ways." He tipped his hat and took off at a run in the opposite direction through the murky underground, vanishing in less than a second.

Only sheer willpower kept Andrea from screaming out in terror. She knew that somehow Vanessa was behind this little trick. She had to be. Who else would plan such a mean joke? Andrea had to reluctantly admit that it was good though. A great prank, but enough was enough. She wanted back into the well-lit safety of the restaurant with the rest of her crazy, fun-loving relatives. She turned, massaging her aching head, and began to walk in the direction she hoped the restaurant was located. She inched along – her hands reaching out to touch the rough walls on either side. It felt dank and it crumbled in places, causing little pebbles to fall at her feet. They made a crunching noise as she shuffled along. It echoed hauntingly, reverberating off the narrow walls, reminding her of how very much alone she was.

There were only the two ways to go, and since the boy had taken off in the other direction, Andrea felt pretty certain that she was heading the right way. She felt her way along the wall, feeling the dampness seep into her running shoes. This place gives me the creeps, she thought. Was this part of Vanessa's planned revenge too? To make her a bundle of nerves for the wedding tomorrow? Was her whole family in on this? They must be, she thought, though she had never known her parents to be cruel before. And this being alone in such a terrifying place was cruel indeed. Andrea shivered as she heard a scurrying sound above her head. She forced herself not to think about what it might be and kept moving. This joke had a nightmarish quality to it. It was chock full of everything Andrea feared: darkness, solitude, and unknown creatures.

Andrea's imagination finally won over her mind. Pictures of all sorts of spooky, horrid creatures flooded her brain. Fear climbed up her throat and jumped out her open mouth.

"Vanessa!" she yelled. "You win this time! Just get me out of here! Vanessa!"

She'd barely finished yelling when a grimy hand clamped over her mouth. It was the strange boy again. "Stop screaming!" he thundered in her ear. "Or we'll get found out." Andrea squirmed and wriggled, trying to free herself from his grasp. He was strong and refused to release his hold. "Ya gonna stop screamin' now?" he asked, not unkindly, still holding her in a death squeeze.

Andrea nodded, more calm now that she realized

that she was no longer alone. The boy slowly released her, standing close enough to grab her again if she called out. Or maybe he was trying to see Andrea more clearly in the dim light that managed to seep into the gloomy tunnel. "Wh-where am I?" she squeaked, gagging slightly at the feel of grime and dirt on her lips. She wiped her mouth on her shirt sleeve.

"Why, you're near The Four Star Café, I'd reckon."

"Look, just take me back to where you met me, then I'll be able to find my own way back to the restaurant."

"I ain't got time to take you anywhere but to the Station. The train's due any minute and I got a job to do, see. So do you," he admonished her, "and you'd better take it. Pays real well – if you got the guts for it." He looked Andrea up and down contemptuously as if seriously doubting that she had what it took to do the job. "Ya look too much like a girl," he scowled scornfully. "Too soft in the face. Better toughen up a bit if you know what's good for ya. Boy, ya gotta be tough in this business." He took off his cap and tossed it in her direction. "Here, wear this. It'll help ya look more boy-like." He turned away and then whirled around again. "What's your name?"

"Andr-And-Andy," Andrea stuttered. She'd suddenly realized that "Andrea" was not the kind of name he was expecting to hear. He didn't want to know that his newest charge was indeed female. He'd probably abandon her right here in this horrible tunnel, and how would she ever find her way out again?

"Andy. I'm Vance." He extended his grimy hand once again, this time in friendship, and squeezed her small hand in a vise grip of welcome. His arm came up to clumsily pat her shoulder. "Don't worry none 'bout all yer yellin' and carryin' on. I seen bigger an' older guys than you carry on even worse. This job ain't for everyone, see. Ya gotta be able to stand the dark and the feeling of being close." He smiled a ghost of a smile then cleared his throat noisily, as if suddenly uncomfortable. "Now, follow me. We're headin' to the Station." He spoke brusquely and disappeared into the darkness.

Andrea jammed the hat on her head, trying to force her blonde hair up underneath it. She felt her barrettes, still securely attached. Oh bother, she thought, pulling the offending things from her hair and stuffing them into the pocket of her overalls. It was a good thing it was dark. If Vance had seen them, he would have left her in the terrifying tunnels alone and never looked back.

The tunnel was small and dark. Once Andrea felt something fall on her cap. Instinctively her arm reached up to investigate, but her runaway imagination caused her to stop in mid-reach. She really didn't want to know what was up there, especially if it was giant spiders, rats, or bats…. She forced her mind away from those terrifying thoughts.

It smelled mouldy and musty, like a dirty, stinky basement. Every now and again a weak and sputtering kerosene lantern flickered, sending tepid waves of light in both directions for a few metres. That was the only source of light.

The tunnel was so small that Andrea could have, had she so desired, easily touched both walls at once, with her arms spread wide. Where was she? Why was she here? Where was Vanessa and her family? Were they all laughing and having a good joke at her expense, watching her meekly follow this Vance character through the dark tunnels under downtown Moose Jaw? That was it! Somehow Vanessa and her friends had managed to hook up a video camera and were busily filming every scream and shudder.

Andrea wanted to believe that. She desperately wanted to convince herself, to hold that thought, even though she knew that a camera would need much more light to get a clear picture than the quivering, intermittent lamps gave out. But, if not Vanessa, then who or what was behind all of this? Andrea didn't want to speculate.

She kept up the façade as they walked quickly through the stinky tunnel. How much did they pay Vance to play his part? Andrea honestly didn't think her parents or her grandparents would carry a joke this far, not when she was petrified beyond belief, following a kid she didn't know, to who knew where.

But if this wasn't the mega-trick of all time, hosted by Cousin Vanessa, then what was going on?! Andrea didn't want to think about the alternative....

They moved quickly through the tunnels toward the train station. Andrea was getting accustomed to the dimness and was actually able to see better. "Why are we going to the train station?" she asked Vance.

He sighed impatiently. "We got a job to do."

"What kind of job?"

"Ya'll find out once we get there. They don't never give out too much information – it's safer that way, see?"

No. Andrea didn't see, and she wondered why he talked funny, like a mobster wannabe from one of the old, old movies she'd seen on TV. Oh well, she wouldn't be hanging around Vance for too much longer. She knew where the train station was located in Moose Jaw. Who didn't? It was the huge building that stood at the very end of Main Street, causing all traffic to turn right or left onto Manitoba Street. Built in 1922, it was immense and awe inspiring, overlooking the down-town core of the city.

Once they safely reached the train station, Andrea would find a way up to the surface and head, at a run, back to the restaurant. She would casually walk down the stairs and greet her family with great dignity. She wouldn't let them know how worried and afraid she had been, even if they did have it all on video. And, naturally, she'd start planning her revenge, some awesome practical joke that involved every single member of her extended family. She would show no mercy! Even she had to admit, though, that she'd never be able to top this practical joke. Never in a million years. But that was her plan, and she felt better, just hanging on to that fragile thread of hope.

Andrea and Vance could hear the train station even before they actually reached the hidden door in the tunnel wall. There was a low hum of voices and foot traffic busily moving back and forth across the station floor. The louder, more powerful thrum of engines could also be heard. "We're gonna be late!" Vance muttered. He sprinted through an almost hidden door in the side of the tunnel, disappearing entirely right before Andrea's eyes.

"Where are you?" Andrea called out in a panicky voice; then she saw the door. It was cut roughly, perhaps even hacked out, and was easily missed in the dimness.

An arm coiled out of the wall and pulled her into a claustrophobic room. It was very dark and felt cramped and small. "Shh," Vance warned. "We don't wanna be found here."

"Where are we?" Andrea insisted. The room was crowded. She was almost standing on top of Vance, the toes of their shoes slightly overlapping. All around stood shovels, mops and brooms, and two huge drums that probably contained a cleaning solution. It was obviously a caretaker's storeroom.

"All right," Vance muttered. "Let me tell ya the layout – but not here. I'm going to the Men's Room. Know where that is?" Andrea was silent and Vance sighed. "Ya ain't from around here, are ya?" Reluctantly, Andrea made a negative sound. "It always helps ta have boys who know the town." He sighed and scratched his head, looking heavenward for help.

"Outside this door is some stairs, see. They go up on one side to the train station, or up the other to the tracks. The Men's Room is across the station and to the right. Ya can't miss it, and it'll be busy. I'm gonna leave first, see? You give me three minutes and then follow me to the Men's Room. We can talk there."

"Wh-why the Men's Room?" Andrea questioned. That was the last place she wanted to go! Not the Men's Room! Please, anywhere but there. "Wh-why not just the-the benches?" She remembered seeing old photographs of the interior of the train station in which long wooden benches were situated in the centre of the large area.

"We don't wanna be seen – it's too risky."

"B-but –" Andrea's protest went unheard, for Vance had quietly shuffled his way around the caretaking supplies and disappeared out the door and onto the stairs. Bright light flooded briefly into the room, blinding Andrea and then leaving her in total darkness again when the door closed behind him. It didn't matter, anyway, Andrea thought. She didn't need to meet Vance at all. She now knew where she was and she was going to head back to the restaurant above ground right now.

Andrea carefully turned around, avoiding the mops and buckets, and made her way to the door. She didn't know why she should be quiet, but something told her that being discovered hiding in this tiny room was not a good idea. She opened the door a crack and peered out, looking for an opportunity to join the throng of people unobserved and head up the stairs and into the station. What she noticed was the yellow light of the primitive light bulbs on the walls. They looked elegant, but did they really provide adequate lighting for the stairs, she wondered. Someone should do something about that. She thought about the safety of the people moving on the stairs and wondered why they weren't using the big bright halogen and fluorescent lights that malls and hotels used for lighting. That would make so much more sense. Why set yourself up for a lawsuit just for the sake of elegance and authenticity? A niggling little thought popped unbidden into Andrea's mind. Maybe this was all the technology they had at the time. Maybe this was the best they could do. Andrea rapidly pushed that thought away. She didn't dare even consider that absurd idea.

The dress of the women, as they swept past the tiny room, caused Andrea to moan and lean heavily against the door. Every woman who passed by was dressed in a prim dress with pleated skirts, huge bows, or large polka dots. The dresses were flashy, designed, Andrea thought, to get attention. And they all wore hats! And little white gloves. No woman Andrea knew wore hats and gloves like that. And the men. Almost all of them wore suits, or vests and dress pants. They wore baggy dress slacks and polka dot ties! Where were the jeans and cutoffs and running shoes? Oh, what was going on? Again Andrea tried unsuccessfully to push horrid and totally freakish thoughts out of her mind. Had she really slipped back in time, or was this all a terrible, horrible nightmare?

Was she actually back in Moose Jaw in the 1920s? What had Mr. Saunders said about the tunnels? Andrea had to admit that she really hadn't been all that interested and so hadn't paid much attention. Now she wished that she had. Panic grabbed hold of her stomach and shook it. She had to do something! She had to know for absolutely certain what was going on. She burst out of the room, letting the door crash against the wall behind her. Luckily very few people looked up as she sprinted the stairs to the station two and three at a time and pushed the heavy glass and wooden frame door open at the top. It was only a short distance across the marble floor of the train station to the front entrance, but Andrea felt as if she had run miles. Her heart pounded loudly in her chest as she leaned on the heavy door and half fell, half ran into the evening air.

7:30 PM Friday Night

LITTLE CHICAGO?

Andrea looked up Main Street and stopped short at the sight. Gone were the cars zooming up and down only a few short minutes before; gone were the traffic lights blinking red and green to control the flow of vehicles; gone too were many of the buildings she was used to seeing. Instead Andrea saw a few horses and buggies. And cars! The Model T kind she had seen at the Western Development Museum, and ancient looking street lights with huge glass globes. She wrapped her arms around her midriff to keep from shaking. What was going on? It must be a joke, it must be a joke, Andrea repeated over and over in her mind, like a chant, as she stared unbelieving at the scene before her eyes. She shook her head a few times as if to clear it, but the town remained, smaller, older, and almost unrecognizable in her eyes. Andrea felt tears begin to threaten and knew that wouldn't help her at all. She wasn't a crybaby at the worst of times, and even though this was really bad, she refused to give in to tears. So she had gone back in time; other people had done it like...like in the movies. But this was real life! What was she to do? Andrea absolutely rejected the idea that she was stuck in the 1920s forever. There had to be some way back to the present and to her family – and she intended to find it.

HOW LONG SHE STOOD THERE GAWKING at the town gone awry, Andrea could not say. People brushed by her, politely excusing themselves and hurrying off into the evening sun. Andrea finally gave herself a mental shake. Standing rooted to one spot in front of the train station would only bring attention to herself. The best thing to do, she decided, was to stay with Vance, but to do that, she would have to brave the Men's Room and go in search of him. Resolutely, Andrea turned back to the station.

She found the Men's Room along the outer wall of the train station, its windows facing Manitoba Street. A huge doorway led into the facility, and with great reluctance Andrea allowed her feet to march her inside. She let her mind go blank, preparing herself for any strange sights she might encounter. There were two rooms, she discovered as soon as she'd crossed the threshold of the main doorway. One room was obviously the place for relieving oneself and, with a huge sigh of gratitude, Andrea avoided that room totally. The other room appeared to be a smoking and sitting room of sorts. Andrea decided to try there first. She stepped to her right and entered the sitting room. Large couches and armchairs were scattered around, as well as a table where a few men sat talking quietly. They glanced up as she entered and she froze for a moment, wondering if they would guess that she was female and definitely in the wrong place.

"Psst." Andrea heard and turned back toward the sound to discover Vance waving wildly at her from the doorway. "Come on," he urged. "We ain't got time now. Gotta meet the train from Chicago. Just follow me, I'll teach ya the ropes!" He disappeared out the door and into the busy train station.

Andrea had trouble keeping up with him as he darted back down the stairs to the underpass and then up the other stairs to the platform where a train was just pulling into the station. Andrea watched as a thin, pale man approached Vance and talked rapidly. Vance nodded several times and jerked his head in Andrea's direction. The man watched her rather unwilling approach, looking her up and down several times.

"You'll do," he pronounced. "Listen to the boy," he muttered, jerking a thumb in Vance's direction. "He's one of the best. Stick with him, kid, and you'll learn a lot."

The man stepped back into the shadows leaving Andrea and Vance alone on the platform. "What are we doing here?" she whispered frantically.

"We gotta carry the passengers to certain spots, see."

"Carry?!"

"Shh! Here they come now." Andrea watched as six men came slowly down the length of the platform. They had obviously just gotten off the train. Even with Andrea's modern taste in clothing, she could tell that these gentlemen were well dressed. They wore white baggy trousers and white hats and blue or black dinner jackets and shiny shoes. But who were they?

Vance whistled appreciatively as he watched the men approach. "Boy, somethin' big's goin' on in this town tanight. I ain't seen guys like this come ta town in a long, long time. It's gonna be a hot time in the ol' town tanight." He half sang the old song under his breath as they drew near.

"Who are th-they?" Andrea stuttered. "What's going to happen?" Her questions fell on deaf ears.

"Just follow me, Andy," Vance ordered as the men stopped in the shadow of the train station, "and *don't* ask so many questions! I'm gonna take one group back into the tunnel. You follow in three minutes with the other group. I'll wait for you just up the tunnel and show you how it's done."

"B-but," Andrea sputtered, "w-wouldn't it be much easier to just use the street?"

Vance laughed and clapped Andrea hard on the back, causing her to lurch forward, almost losing her balance. "That's cute, Andy. Real cute. That's the best joke I've heard in a long time. Use the street!" Vance was still chuckling to himself as he stepped back into the shadows and motioned the men to follow him. It was almost as if he, too, didn't want to be seen. Even though they were not looking directly at Vance, the men somehow got the signal, for they fell in a few paces behind Vance, following at a distance.

Andrea watched as they disappeared into the doors that led down into the underpass to the station. This was very, very fishy. What did the men want, and where was Vance taking them? Oh, what had Mr. Saunders said about the tunnels? Andrea racked her brain trying to remember.... She drew a blank. Nothing. It was almost as bad as when she studied really hard for her French verb tests and then blew it because she couldn't remember a thing.

Andrea saw the men hesitate and gather in a group to discuss something, before they vanished from sight. Why weren't they using the stairs into the station, unless they were doing something illegal and didn't want to be seen! Why were they disappearing into the tiny room she had only just vacated? Andrea didn't like the feel of this. These men were smooth, very smooth. She was sure that she was the only person on the platform who knew what had happened to them and where they had gone.

Shaking in her damp running shoes, Andrea waited the appropriate amount of time, then discreetly signalled the last three men. They too appeared to ignore her, yet she sensed their presence as she slid through the heavy door. They followed her down the stairs to the underpass and paused at the bottom of the long flight of steps that led up to the station. It didn't make any sense to her that these men wanted to go through those dirty horrid little tunnels. What, oh what had Mr. Saunders said about the tunnels...she wished she could remember. Andrea glanced around to make sure no one was watching and then quickly pushed open the door to the caretaking room and stepped inside.

The cool darkness was almost welcome. Andrea squeezed into the furthest corner of the room while the men followed her. Three adults and a child in the small room seemed impossible, and yet they all managed to fit. When the last man was in and the door quietly shut, Andrea felt a moment of panic. What if she couldn't find the hidden entrance to the tunnel? Think, Andrea, think! Where was it? Behind the large barrel near the shovel that was leaning into the corner of the room. She remembered having to step carefully around the shovel so as not to knock it over.

Andrea slid against the wall near the drum of cleaning solution and found the shovel. Reaching her hand around behind it, she encountered cold cement. It didn't seem possible that there was a passageway here. Then her hand felt a cool, faint draft filtering in through a narrow crack in the wall. It must be coming from the tunnels. She gave a slight push against the wall and the door slid open. Andrea lost her balance and stumbled into the darkness of the tunnel.

The three men followed quickly behind her, the last one carefully shutting the secret door. Meanwhile, Andrea struck out in the darkness, heading in the only direction she could go, hoping that Vance, true to his word, would be waiting for her just up ahead. If he wasn't, she didn't know what she would do!

The men hurried behind her as if part of a bizarre game of Follow-The-Leader, or perhaps Blindman's Bluff. Andrea stifled a giggle at the thought of leading the men on a wild goose chase all night. After all, she sure didn't know where she was or where she was going!

Andrea was getting more frightened by the minute. She wondered if Vance was truly waiting for her. Then she heard the scuffle of feet ahead. It had to be Vance. Who else would be scurrying along in these dark, scary tunnels? In the light of a lantern burning weakly ahead, Andrea recognized Vance's plaid shirt just barely visible in front of the three men he was leading. She followed along closely, not wanting to be left behind. She couldn't figure out how Vance knew just where to go. It must have something to do with the lanterns, she decided. She almost ran into a pole in the middle of the tunnel. The tunnels appeared to be laid out like the grid of streets above them, branching out at right angles at each intersection. Some tunnels, Andrea noticed, were very small indeed, and she wondered what they were used for. Perhaps they hadn't been hollowed out enough, she thought, glad that they hadn't tried to navigate any of those.

Suddenly Vance and the three men with him disappeared. Andrea couldn't believe her eyes. Quickly, she moved to the spot she'd seen them last. She saw a tunnel that led away to the left, and there they were, already quite far down it. She quickly followed, and almost caught up to them.

All at once, Vance and the three men ahead of her stopped. Andrea, who had been woolgathering, almost collided with the man in front of her. She managed to stop in time, her nose just brushing the itchy wool of his dinner jacket. He smelled of cheap, overpowering cologne and cigars, a combination that almost turned Andrea's stomach. She quickly stepped back a pace, crunching the toes of the man behind her under the heel of her foot.

"Sorry," she muttered as she heard him utter a curse under his breath. It was a word that would have caused her father to turn beet red and her mother to lecture the guy for at least a half hour on his choice of language.

"Watch the patent leather, buddy!" the miffed man ground out between clenched teeth. "These are brand new shoes."

"Sorry," Andrea muttered again.

Vance tapped lightly on what appeared to be a dirt wall. Andrea was sure that he had lost his marbles until a soft knock in code-like precision tapped back. Vance replied with another knock and the wall moved inward, dim light spilling out into the tunnel. "All cargo safe and accounted for," Vance reported to the man at the door. The well-dressed older man opened the door more widely, allowing the men in the tunnel to slip silently past him. There would be time for a more jovial greeting after the tunnel door was once again safely secured. Vance waited expectantly and was not disappointed. When the last man had disappeared inside, the doorman neatly flipped a silver coin into the air. Vance deftly caught and smoothly pocketed it almost before Andrea realized what was happening. The door started to slide back into place when the man noticed Andrea standing in the shadows.

"New guy?"

Vance nodded. "Yep, I'm trainin' him."

"Well, share your wealth with him." The door slid shut completely, blocking out the dim light and leaving Andrea with the now familiar panicky feeling of claustrophobia rising in her throat.

The darkness didn't bother Vance – he was still concerned about the money. "Aw come on," he argued with the closed door, "give us a break here. This is hard work!"

A soft laugh floated eerily into the tunnel. "Go cry at someone else's door, kid, your work's done here."

Vance was obviously annoyed as he reached into his pocket to feel the lone coin once more. He frowned into the darkness. Andrea stared at Vance wide-eyed, a mysterious feeling of déjà vu washing over her. She had seen that exact action of hand to pocket at least a hundred times before, but she couldn't place it.

Vance had other thoughts on his mind. He took a menacing step toward Andrea, his fists clenched at his sides. He looked ready to fight for a lousy coin. "I-I don't want the money," Andrea stammered, taking a step backward. She was afraid that Vance would be very angry at having to share the money and would leave her down in the tunnels.

Vance laughed cynically. "Everybody wants dough!" Andrea solemnly shook her head and Vance turned to look suspiciously at her. "We all need dough, see," he stated roughly. "What makes you different? Or have you got a stash of your own hidden somewhere?" Looking as if he were going to shake the answer out of her, he took a threatening step toward her.

Suddenly Andrea felt afraid. Really afraid. Here she was, all alone in the dark tunnel with a boy she knew nothing about. She had put her trust in a stranger, hoping that he would help her. She was all alone in this strangely warped world with a peculiar boy who was acting more bizarre by the minute. A saving thought jumped into Andrea's mind and she blurted, "Really – I-I don't want your money, and n-no," she spoke rapidly, "I don't have any money – I-I just th-thought my share was g-going to your training me for the j-job t-t-tonight."

Vance regarded her through narrowed eyes, as if trying to figure out if Andy was for real. Suddenly he smiled and clapped her on the back, his cheerful mood restored. "Sure, kid. Sure. That's what the money's for – me trainin' ya. And I'll give you the best trainin' ever," he declared. He turned Andrea back toward the lantern sputtering on a pole twenty metres away. "We've got a few minutes, let's get started now. You'll be rakin' in your own dough by the end of the night!"

Under the yellow light of the lantern, Vance squatted down and picked up a small jagged rock from the dirt floor. He proceeded to scratch straight lines into the packed earth. The tunnels, Andrea learned, were basically on the grid system, as she had suspected. At least as much as possible. There were some that twisted and turned, but mainly the tunnels had been dug from site A to site B – as straight as possible. Andrea figured that this must be to make it easier to keep a sense of direction underground. It sure wouldn't do to have people roaming around the tunnels, lost. She shuddered, thinking of how hungry one might get, not to mention petrified.

The lanterns were markers, letting the guides know where to turn and how far to travel along the dark, confusing mazes. From the train station, it was three lanterns straight to The Four Star Café, where a pole stood in the centre of the tunnel. It must be used for support, Andrea supposed. Just before The Four Star Café, one could turn west and travel another seven lanterns to the Imperial Hotel. To get to Scotty's Shoe Store, one had to head north past The Four Star Café another two lanterns then take a tunnel to the left. The Hazleton Hotel was reached by going past the tunnel to Scotty's Shoe Store, then turning east into the tunnel that crossed Main Street underground, turning north and travelling eight lanterns, then turning east again and travelling another two lanterns.

"I hope you got a good mind," Vance advised as he drew and talked. "Ya'll need it in this business." He continued to sketch in the dirt as Andrea rapidly tried to memorize numbers and places. It was good that she was somewhat familiar with the modern Moose Jaw. It helped her in placing the businesses Vance mentioned. "Now," Vance's voice was suddenly low and serious. "Ya can't ever go into this tunnel." He pointed at the dirt and made a thin line leading north past the Main Street crossing. "It's off limits – forbidden."

"Why?"

Vance sighed in exasperation. "I just knew you was gonna ask that! Just trust me. It's too dangerous. Ol' Scarface'll kill anyone seen in that tunnel without his permission."

"Who's Old Scarface?" Andrea wanted to know.

"Oh, you'll meet 'im," Vance replied. "Just remember, no one uses this tunnel."

"You included?" Andrea wanted to know. She suddenly wondered just what kind of relationship Vance and this Ol' Scarface had. If she was to trust Vance, did that mean she should automatically trust this Scarface too? She wasn't sure she wanted to trust someone with a nickname like that, but she was curious about him.

"Naw," Vance replied. He would have swaggered if he had been standing. "Me 'n Scarface, we sorta got a pact, ya know. I treat him fair and he treats me fair. That's the way it is down here."

Squatting in the darkened tunnel with a virtual stranger, Andrea felt utterly confused and alone. Vance said "trust me," and yet not five minutes before, he had been ready to fight her for a lousy coin. Still, she really didn't have much choice at the moment. Vance seemed somewhat friendly at least, and perhaps he could help keep her safe until she figured out how to get back to the present, if there was a way. That thought scared Andrea and she pushed it far back into her mind. She refused to think about that possibility right now. "How can you kill somebody just for walking through a stupid tunnel?" Andrea wondered aloud.

Vance laughed bitterly. "He'd kill ya for less than that, Andy, if he felt he had reason – wouldn't even need ta be a good reason, neither."

"B-but how can that be?!" It sounded as terrifying as something right out of a fast-paced action movie. Could this be real life?

"That's the way it is 'round here," Vance said flatly. "If ya don't like it, look for work somewheres else." I would, Andrea thought grimly, if I knew how to get out of here. "Just stay out of that tunnel, ya got that?" Vance asked as he stood brushing his hands on the seat of his pants. "That's enough for now," he added. "That's usually all ya need to know, most nights." Vance paused, his eyes shining with excitement. "But tonight it might be different."

"What do you mean?"

"The men we just dropped off look real important. I don't know who they are, but I can tell just by lookin' at 'em," Vance boasted. "They're big shots in the business. I bet they've come from Chicago to check out Ol' Scarface's territory! Maybe they want a little piece of the business. His business! Something big's gonna happen tonight. I can feel it in the air!"

Andrea shivered and wrapped her arms around her ribs. She didn't feel excited at all, with all that fear and panic clawing at her stomach. She closed her eyes, willing herself to stay calm and pay attention. Andrea tried to get a picture of the tunnel system firmly established in her mind for later. The Four Star Café, she figured, was where her parents were having supper at this very moment. If she could just get back there, maybe she would find that this had all been a very bad dream.

"Okay then," Vance said. "You lead."

"Me? Where?" Andrea asked, startled that she had to put her new-found knowledge to the test so quickly.

"We get most of our orders from either that man at the Station or a few other fellas at The Four Star Café. So why don't you head back to the café?" Great! Something was finally working out to her advantage. Here I come, family, Andrea almost crowed with excitement. I'll be back soon. She set off at a brisk pace, Vance dogging her steps every inch of the way.

Miraculously, Andrea found her way back to the restaurant. She wasn't quite sure how she did it, but as she stepped into the dim circle of light made by the weak lamp, Vance clapped her hard on the shoulder. "Ya did it!" he grinned, his even teeth flashing yellow beneath the lantern light. He seemed proud as punch of her success. "This is the pole ya gotta watch out for," he told her, patting the offending shaft where it stood in the centre of the narrow tunnel. "I've crashed into it more than once myself," he added with a laugh, gingerly rubbing his head.

Andrea scarcely heard what Vance said. The Four Star Café! Without stopping to think of the consequences of her actions, Andrea pushed hard against the faint square outline and half-fell, half-stumbled into the basement room. "Don't go in there!" She vaguely heard Vance's astonished cry when he realized what she was doing. She felt his hand grab her shoulder and knew that she would have an unreal bruise on that spot in the morning.

Andrea felt hope flow out of her like air escaping from a broken balloon. Oh, she had so wished that her family would indeed be waiting for her, rejoicing in her safe return. Now, for certain, she knew the truth. She had indeed travelled back in time.

The banquet room had changed over the years. Gone was the noise and conversation of her talkative family; gone too, were all of her relatives. The table, so prominently placed in the centre of the room before, was also missing. In its place stood a smaller wooden games table. The same fancy, crystal-ornamented chandelier hung from the centre of the ceiling. Polished hardwood floorboards replaced the carpet. They creaked as a chair scraped rapidly backward.

"What's going on?!" demanded a man as the chair hit the floor with a resounding bang. He grabbed for a bulge under his jacket that Andrea was sure was a gun.

All other action had frozen the moment Andrea had fallen into the room. One man held a card in mid-play. He had been about to lay it down in the discard pile. It was now frozen in space a few centimetres above the table. The other man had tried to hide a glass of amber-coloured liquid in his suit jacket. It was pressed against his chest, a large wet stain rapidly spreading over the white shirt. This man too, was reaching into his bulging jacket. Did all of these men carry guns?!

"'Scu-'scuse, us, sir," Vance apologised, wringing his hands. From his actions and the incredulous look on his face, Andrea knew that she must have done something terribly wrong. "Th-this here new fella don't know the rules yet," he rapidly explained. "I-I tried to stop him, but I didn't know what he was trying to do."

A stern, almost frightening looking man rose from his chair and walked stiffly over to them. "Mr. Saunders?!" Andrea asked with disbelief. The man looked like Mr. Saunders from The Four Star Café, only he was much younger.

"Huh?!" he questioned. He stopped and stood glaring down at Vance and Andrea. It was his turn to be confused. "Don't go changin' the subject, kid. You're in big trouble!" he sneered, rubbing his smooth chin.

Vance boldly took a step in front of Andrea. "He didn't know no better," Vance pleaded her case. "Give 'im another chance." Vance put a hesitant hand on the man's forearm.

"Don't you ever touch me without permission, boy!" He shook Vance free and knocked him flying against the wall with one sweep of his beefy arm. "I thought you'd learned better 'n' that. Maybe you need another lesson?" It was a quiet question aimed at Vance; quiet but deadly, judging by the steel tone in his voice. "I'll get to you later, boy." He turned his attention back to Andrea.

"Don't know the ropes yet, huh, kid?" He spoke softly, yet Andrea felt chills chase one another up and down her spine. The tiny hairs on the back of her neck stood up in warning. This man was dangerous. Every instinct in her body screamed for her to run, escape before something terrible happened. She stood rooted to the spot. Even if she could run, she had nowhere to go.

"N-no, sir," she heard herself whisper, deciding she had better concentrate on what he was saying. She didn't want to have any more trouble with him. She stared hard at the sparkling white and black patent leather shoes. They were so shiny, she was sure she could see her frozen features mirrored there.

The man took a sinister step toward her, grabbed the back of her head and hair and roughly jerked. It happened so quickly that Andrea didn't have time to dodge. She felt the cap on her head wobble and almost tumble to the floor. Luckily it stayed in place, hiding her true identity. Andrea's head swung up and she found herself staring helplessly into the man's face, tears of pain forming in her eyes. A deep, ugly scar ran down the side of the man's cheek. It was Old Scarface! Andrea was sure of it. Who else would have a scar like that?

"What ya staring at, kid?" he demanded, pulling her hair even more tightly, causing Andrea to rise up on unsteady tiptoes to try to relieve the pain. "Don't like my face job, huh? This'll learn you a lesson!" His eyes glittered angrily. He raised his arm as if to give her a back hand across the mouth, when the clatter of footsteps was heard coming down the steep narrow stairs. A wiry, nervous little man stood waving his arms in agitation, sputtering meaningless words into the blue air. "Well, speak up, man. We ain't got all day!"

"The c-cops are going t-to r-raid Scotty's!" he finally managed to spit out.

"What?!" Scarface released Andrea abruptly. She sank to the floor at his feet, her knees having finally given out from panic and pain. "How do ya know?" Old Scarface shouted.

"C-coffee. They w-were having coffee here and let it slip out. I overheard 'em!"

Scarface thumped a beefy, mean-looking fist into the palm of his other hand. "We gotta do something!" He glanced at Andrea, still cowering on the floor and his eyebrows suddenly shot upward. "You!" he yelled, grabbing her once again by the hair. "You owe me for busting into this joint uninvited like that." He dragged her across the room and pulled the armoire roughly away from the wall. It creaked and groaned from the sudden movement, almost falling from its hinges. "In there now!"

Where, Andrea wondered. The tunnel that she and Vance had just used was on the opposite end of the room. Only a small hole was visible in the dirt wall behind the shiny armoire. It looked like the start of a tunnel; one that hadn't been completely hollowed out yet. "In-in there?!" Andrea whispered, disbelieving. Even in her worst nightmares, she had never been subjected to the mortal terror he was now suggesting. "I-I c-c-can't," she murmured, but her words were lost in the shuffling noises of the gravel under their feet.

Somehow Vance had found his way to her side. "It's okay, Andy," he whispered as he grabbed her arm, pretending to help direct her into the black hole of doom. "This tunnel leads to Scotty's. Crawl as fast as you can. You must get there to warn them in time! That's the only way to get out of his bad books." He jerked a thumb in Scarface's direction.

They had reached the small opening in the dirt. Old Scarface bodily picked Andrea up and shoved her into the void. She fell to her hands and knees inside and looked back over her shoulder just in time to see Scarface slam the armoire closed, leaving Andrea in total and complete suffocating blackness. "Hurry, boy! You'd better make it in time, or else!"

8:55 PM Friday Night

TERROR UNDERGROUND

Andrea was a petrified fossil, frozen in place in the minuscule tunnel. They expected her to crawl – crawl in pitch blackness all the way to the shoe store – just to warn some gangsters that the cops were coming! Let the cops get them. She didn't care, she only knew that there was no way she was crawling, walking, running, or even flying through this narrow, crude passageway they called a tunnel. The "real" tunnels were bad enough. She could barely manage to keep her wits about her in them. How could she possibly control her imagination in this situation? *I'd rather die*, Andrea silently vowed. Her panting breath was muffled by the closeness of the damp earth only centimetres above her head.

"No, I wouldn't rather die," she recanted slowly, realising that she basically had two choices. She could stay in the tunnel and let the gangsters get caught. She was sure to suffer the wrath of Old Scarface if she did that. Or she could crawl for all she was worth, hoping to beat the cops to Scotty's in time to warn the men to hide! What kind of choice was that?! It wasn't a choice. The decision had been made the second Scarface had shoved her into the tunnel.

Well, then, I'd better make it, Andrea decided grimly, and she set off on her hands and knees, crawling over rocks and large clumps of dirt. In the space of a few metres her knees stung, her hands were scratched and cut. Cobwebs hung low and slapped her in the face as she passed. Andrea shut her eyes and gritted her teeth. Don't think about it, Andrea willed as her imagination began to work overtime. But thoughts of spiders, immense and hairy, with grotesque faces, began to haunt her thoughts.

The narrow space was suddenly enlarged enough so that Andrea could stand, crouched over, and run. This she did, glad to be able to move more swiftly. The darkness though, was airless and stifling. She felt something thump her softly on the back and roll off. She screamed and then clamped her own dirty hand over her mouth. There was no telling if the sound would travel or not, but Andrea didn't want to take any chances.

The journey felt endless. She was in a black hole of eternity. There was no exit and she was lost, doomed to starvation and certain death. Stop it! Andrea willed. Don't panic. She forced her mind to think of other things: the mountains, fresh and open; the sun shining on the beautiful river back home. Stay calm, she encouraged herself silently, you can do this.

The tunnel curved. In the darkness Andrea couldn't see the turn. She ran into the side of the dirt wall. Part of it caved in, falling on her back and shoulders. Vance's hat threatened to jiggle loose on her head and she quickly jammed it back into place. She ran on; she'd worry about the dirt later. Would this blackness never end?

But soon it did, for just up ahead Andrea could suddenly see a whisper of light escaping from a small hole. She stumbled and fell, picked herself up and ran on, her eyes never straying from the deliverance of light ahead.

The light grew larger and more bright as Andrea closed in on it. It was actually a vent at waist level. Andrea bent down and peered breathlessly into the lighted area on the other side. It was the basement of the shoe store, of that she was certain! There were boxes of shoes everywhere, and tools and equipment that Andrea thought must be used for repairing and making shoes. The six men they had delivered earlier were there, along with two others and several women.

A card game was obviously in progress, and judging by the pile of money in the centre of the table, there was gambling as well.

All of this Andrea noted in a matter of seconds. Now that she had reached her destination, she did not want to fail by forgetting to warn the people. "Hey," she called out weakly. She felt stupid and silly calling from outside of the room.

"Did you hear something?" one of the women asked suspiciously.

Everyone went stiff and still, as if they were expecting trouble of some sort.

"Hey!" Andrea called more loudly this time. "Over here, in the vent!"

Two men jumped up from the table and quickly removed the vent cover. Andrea fairly leaped the metre or so down to the basement floor. It felt like paradise after her horrifying trip through that tunnel. "The cops are coming! There's going to be a raid!"

"Raid!" They all shouted and jumped into action. The two men forced the vent cover back into place as a woman swept up the dirt that had slid in with Andrea. Another large cupboard, not unlike the one in the café, was slid open, revealing a large hiding space. It looked as if it had originally been a small storage area. It now stood empty, ready to hide the fugitives from the police. The men, carrying their alcoholic beverages, cards, and money, scurried into the hollowed-out space and were quickly joined by the women.

"Come on!" one of them shouted to Andrea. "Get in here, quick!" Andrea raced across the room and into the crowded space just as the pounding of feet was heard on the wooden floor above. Two men remained outside and shoved the cupboard closed, cleverly concealing the people hidden behind.

Noisy feet clattered down the stairs and burst into the basement room. "This is a raid!" one of the cops shouted as they skidded to a stop in the silent room.

In the concealed area behind the cupboard, Andrea held her breath, barely daring to breathe. She was squashed tightly between a short, rotund man who smelled of cigar smoke and a heavily perfumed lady in feathers and fancy clothes. It was almost as suffocating as being in the horrid hole misnamed a tunnel by the overzealous bad guys. Feathers tickled Andrea's nose and she squeezed her eyes shut firmly, willing herself not to sneeze. That would ruin everything! She wondered what they would do with a child her age caught in an illegal situation like this. Did children go to prison in those days, she wondered. She didn't want to be around to discover what would happen.

Every sound, every word, was clearly heard by those hidden behind the cupboard. They listened to the police clump around in their heavy boots, demanding to know where the liquor was hidden. Cupboard doors were clapped open and then slammed shut in the search for illicit material. It seemed as if every inch of the place would be searched.

"Come on, Scotty!" one of the uniformed men demanded. "'Fess up! We know something's been going on around here!"

"Look, I'm just repairing these shoes, see? And old Joe here is visitin'. Is there a law against that now too?"

"Got nothin' else to do on a Friday night?" a police officer jeered.

"What's to do in Moose Jaw?" the man named Joe whined.

That's what I would have said, until now, Andrea thought, amazed by the turn of events in her life. Moose Jaw should be just a boring small city on the bald prairie. None of this should be happening.

Andrea shifted slightly, trying to get more space, and discovered that there was a small crack between the armoire and the wall. She could just see the sleeve of an officer's uniform as he paused near the cupboard.

Don't touch! Andrea begged silently. The cop dragged open a drawer in the very cupboard that screened the hiding place. It shook slightly and creaked. The whole group held its breath in terror. "Nothing!" he confirmed after a few seconds. The collective group behind the cupboard sighed in relief.

The police spent what felt like hours scouring the basement of Scotty's Shoe Store, berating and questioning the two men. As they moved toward the stairs that would take them back up to the shoe store and out onto Main Street, the hidden group began to relax. There was more movement as they tried to get comfortable, and quiet sighs could be heard. The man nearest Andrea shuffled his feet and planted one firmly on top of Andrea's shoe. He almost lost his balance and instinctively put out his hands to steady himself. Unfortunately, he was the man who had scooped up most of the money from the table. A coin jarred itself loose from his grasp and clattered to the floor and began to roll. In the silence of the basement, the clinking of the coin sounded like thunder to Andrea's hypersensitive ears. She listened in horror as it rolled out from under the armoire, her breath caught in her throat. The coin travelled in a lazy circle, finally coming to a stop with one last clink against the hardwood floor.

"What was that?!" the chief officer demanded. Andrea could see his profile through her small vantage point. His beady eyes darted this way and that and came to rest on the cupboard behind which the small group of people was concealed. He took one step and then another in the direction of the armoire staring at it suspiciously. The group held its breath, as frozen as statues in Crescent Park. Andrea shuddered when she saw him reach his hand out to touch the cupboard.

Suddenly the sound of rain could be heard in the basement. "What was what?" Scotty asked innocently above the sound. Andrea strained to one side. She could just see Scotty holding a shoe and hammer. He bent and was lost from her sight for a second and a scraping noise could be heard. "Sorry," he apologised to the constables. "Just dropped my nails."

The cop took one last look at the cupboard, muttered an expletive and turned away. "We'll get you one of these days, Scotty! You mark my words!"

Scotty laughed. "I ain't got nothin' ta hide," he declared with a grin.

"Let's not waste any more time here," the cop said. "There's a rumour Ol' Scarface himself is in town tonight. He's the big cheese. Let's concentrate on him!" The cops clattered noisily up the stairs, leaving the basement room in silence.

There they all stayed, shut up in the airless room for what seemed like forever, while Scotty hummed to himself and worked on a pair of tattered and torn ladies boots. Joe whistled under his breath, propped on a chair that leaned against the wall. He flipped rather quickly through an old magazine. "You're turning the pages too fast," Scotty finally admonished. "Besides, everyone knows you can't read!"

"Nope," Joe agreed cheerfully. "Never went to school!"

"Then, what are ya doing!?"

"Just trying to look in-ino-" he scratched his head, suddenly at a loss for the right word.

"Innocent," Scotty supplied in annoyance.

"Think we can let 'em out now?" Joe whispered behind his magazine.

"Soon," Scotty replied. "I just wanna make sure that they're really gone."

"Go upstairs and get me some more nails," Scotty demanded loudly. "And leave the lights off," he whispered behind his hand.

"What for?" Joe wanted to know. "How can I find anything in the dark?"

"That's just an excuse, if yer caught up there," Scotty whispered. "What you're really doin' is seein' if they're all gone!"

"Oh-h-h!" Joe smiled conspiratorially and let the chair down with a thump. "Ya need some nails, ya say, Scotty? I'll go fetch 'em for ya." Joe stretched slowly and then walked close to the armoire. "I'll let ya out soon as I go check upstairs." He tapped lightly on the cupboard and then stomped noisily upstairs.

Joe finally returned with the all clear and Scotty opened the cupboard door. Fresh cool air rushed in to greet the cramped individuals. They stumbled out stretching and groaning. "That was a close call!" the short man said.

"No thanks to George," Scotty retorted, pointing to the man who still held the money clutched against his chest. "It's a good thing I saw that coin before the cops did and poured my nails all over the floor or we all woulda been in jail."

"Thanks, kid!" one of the ladies smiled. She came close and gave Andrea a big hug, pressing her coloured lips against Andrea's dirt-streaked cheek.

"That's enough, Rosie," the short, fat man admonished. "Save it for Scarface. He'll be askin' to see ya before too long."

Rosie pouted, but released Andrea, patting her cap back into place. "You're such a cute boy," she breathed, pinching Andrea's other cheek. "I'll be sure to tell Al that you did a good job!"

Andrea moved back, uncomfortable with a stranger being so affectionate toward her. As she backed against the wall of the room, her foot gently kicked something. It was the offending coin that had dropped to the floor, almost getting them captured. Swiftly Andrea bent and picked it up, pocketing it almost as smoothly as she had seen Vance do. Won't he be proud of me, she thought, smiling to herself. She was proud of herself as well. Proud that she had traversed the tiny tunnel and kept her wits about her. She couldn't wait to tell Vance all about her first adventure alone!

"Here, kid." The man who had dropped the money in the first place threw another coin in Andrea's direction. "You better head back to Ol' Scarface and let him know what happened. He'll be waitin' to hear."

"Sure thing! But this time I'll use the regular tunnels. After all, it ain't no emergency." Now I'm even talking like them, Andrea thought with annoyance as she waited for Joe to let her out. I'd better be careful or I may decide that I even like being a tunnel rat!

Joe listened quietly at the tunnel entrance for a moment, making sure that it was safe. Andrea was very surprised that the police hadn't found the entrance and tunnel beyond, even though they were very well camouflaged by the wood décor of the basement room. Joe opened the door a crack, leaving just enough room for Andrea to squeeze out into the tunnel from under his arm. "Be careful," he warned. He winked at Andrea and started to shut the door. "Oh, and tell Scarface that Rosie's dying to see him, hear? I'm sure he'll want to see her at the Hazleton tonight." He smiled a sly toothy grin at Andrea and shut the door.

That cold shivering feeling returned, running up Andrea's spine. There was another man she didn't trust. Something about Joe didn't quite add up, but Andrea didn't have time to think about that now, she had to get back to The Four Star Café quickly.

The tunnel seemed much more friendly this time, light even, and somewhat airy, after the gopher hole she had last travelled through. Andrea almost skipped along as she hurried toward The Four Star Café. She felt more confident in the darkness, although she would have preferred to travel above ground like a normal person. She wondered what was going on in the world above her head. Were people walking overhead right now on the streets of Moose Jaw? Was it raining? What would they think of the hidden tunnels right under their feet?!

Andrea did have to admit that it was almost fun having this adventure with Vance and the racketeers, if only she could eventually get home again. It would be terrible to be stuck here forever. No more mountain biking, she thought morosely, no more videos and video games, no more computers and Internet. What would the world be like without all those things? Tough, Andrea decided. It would be tough to live without all of the luxuries that she had grown up with. But toughest, she knew, would be to never see her family again. Sure, she fought with them at times and sometimes even thought that she hated them. The truth was, Andrea was quite close to her family and would really miss them. Even pesky Cousin Richard, she had to reluctantly admit. He didn't seem bad at all when she compared him to Old Scarface and Joe.

The thoughts of her family were making Andrea very sad and she pushed them away to the back of her mind. She knew that she needed to concentrate on navigating the tunnels successfully. Her life depended on her doing a good job and staying on the right side of Ol' Scarface. She would have time to think about her family later.

At the appropriate lantern, Andrea stopped and knocked quietly on the door. She waited, this time, for it to be opened. It took a few moments, but soon the door was swung back to reveal Vance's anxious face. Andrea was so happy to see him, she almost threw her arms around his neck and hugged him. Only the tough expression on his face and the tense way he held his body reminded her that she was supposed to look and act like a boy. Andrea changed her mind at the last second, clapping him clumsily on the shoulder instead. "I made it!" she proclaimed triumphantly. She looked past Vance to Ol' Scarface.

"All safe?" he demanded from the table in the centre of the room. He half rose from the chair, his beady eyes freezing Andrea near the secret door.

Andrea studied him in the dim light. "Yes sir," she replied. "I got there in time and we hid in the secret storage place."

Scarface returned Andrea's gaze for a long moment. "Ya did a good job," he finally admitted. "Didn't think ya had it in ya; thought you was a namby-pamby, but I see I was wrong." A slight smile crinkled the corners of his mouth. A strange smile, Andrea thought, and she wondered why. Then she realized that his eyes were flat, void of all emotion. His lips did a good imitation, but the smile never reached his eyes.

"Th-thanks," Andrea stammered, trying hard not to stare. She searched her exhausted brain for something to say. "Oh!" she suddenly remembered, "R-Rosie's h-hoping to see you t-tonight."

"That so?" Old Scarface questioned. His voice was low and suddenly dangerous again. It caused the hair on Andrea's scalp to prickle in fear. He was inconsistent, Andrea realized, never reacting the same way twice, and that in itself was dangerous. With most people, couldn't you more or less guess how they would react to a given situation? There was safety in knowing how a person might respond.

"I don't see nobody unless I want to see 'em, ya got that?" he said crossly. Andrea nodded and backed slightly away while Scarface made a big show of pulling his expensive pocket watch out of his vest pocket and checking the time.

"I guess I got some time for a little visit." He pointed a fat finger at Vance, who had been standing silently in the corner. "You, go to Scotty's and tell Rosie to meet me in our usual place, got that?"

Vance nodded rapidly. "Yes sir!" he barked, half saluting. Was he mocking Scarface, Andrea wondered, for Vance had a strange glint in his eyes. He looked almost angry. What was going on here? It almost sounded as if Vance was mad at Scarface. Hadn't he told her that they were the best of buddies?

Andrea studied Vance more closely, suddenly noticing that his left eye was puffy and almost swollen shut. It was obviously painful. "Wh-" her lips began to form the words, but no sound was uttered. Vance caught her eye and shook his head once, hard, a warning for her to keep quiet. She turned her head to study Scarface again, suddenly aware of a heavy curtain of tension hanging in the air.

"She'll tell ya where to take her," Scarface continued smoothly. He flipped a coin in the air at Vance, who caught it, pocketed it, and disappeared out into the tunnel as quickly and quietly as a scurrying mole, leaving Andrea feeling totally confused and feeling very vulnerable.

"As for you," Scarface returned his gaze to Andrea, "you are going to take me to the Hazleton, now."

Andrea nodded, already quivering in her wet Reeboks. This was not a game, she realized again. It was a perilous situation of real life that could lead to danger and death at any given moment. The Hazleton Hotel. What had Vance said about it? Andrea tried to concentrate on the job at hand. How did she get there from the café? She couldn't remember where it was located!

Scarface quickly gathered a few belongings and pocketed some loose change on the table. He spoke a few quick words to the wiry man hovering in the corner of the room. The man smiled smugly, glanced in Andrea's direction and nodded. "Whatever you say, boss. Needs to be set straight, he does. Too big for his britches, that one."

Meanwhile Andrea racked her brain trying to remember what Vance had said about the Hazleton. Unfortunately, her exhausted mind refused to co-operate.

"Let's go, kid," Old Scarface commanded, and Andrea felt fear flood her numb limbs.

She slipped from the lighted basement room into the tunnel. The Hazleton. Which way to go? Think, Andrea. Think. Think! Where was the Hazleton?

"What's wrong?!" Scarface demanded.

"N-Nothing," Andrea stuttered. "J-just w-waiting for you, s-sir."

"Well, I'm here now. Get movin'!"

Past the tunnel to Scotty's, Andrea suddenly remembered. She had to go past the tunnel to Scotty's and then turn into the next tunnel that led under Main Street. That was it! With a sigh of relief, she set off.

Andrea nearly felt relaxed, although it was unnerving to have a menacing man following only a short metre behind. She could hear his heavy breathing as they marched along. It gave her goose bumps. What would her parents think, she wondered, if they knew what she was up to? They would be really worried about her, that was certain. They would not approve of her having to associate with a dangerous man like this.

Andrea was careful to keep moving, conscious of trying not to get too far ahead of him. She sure did not want to make him angry. She had seen him angry once, and she didn't want to have that happen again. She wondered for a moment what would have happened if the skinny, nervous man hadn't come shouting down the stairs in The Four Star Café when he did. Would Scarface have really hit her? Andrea was certain of it, and that thought scared her beyond belief.

But had he actually hit Vance? That was the thought she had been trying to avoid thinking. Vance must have run into the pole in the tunnel outside of The Four Star Café; the one he'd warned her to avoid. Ol' Scarface could be mean, but after all he and Vance were buddies, and buddies didn't beat on one another, did they?

Andrea recognized the tunnel to Scotty's right away and realized that she hadn't really been paying attention to where she was going. She slowed down and concentrated on looking for the tunnel that led under Main Street. She found it at a sputtering lamp and turned into the tunnel. It was somewhat narrower and not quite so tall. Her hat brushed the top of the tunnel. Old Scarface must have to stoop, she thought. She reached up to set Vance's cap more firmly on her head. She didn't want to lose it while she had Old Scarface following her; she didn't want him to think, for even one second, that she might be a girl. His wrath would be too much to have to endure.

They plodded on, single file, through the tunnel under the street and then turned north again. How many lanterns did they need to pass? Andrea couldn't remember. This tunnel felt cooler somehow; more breezy. Was that possible? After all, they were all underground. It was as if a giant exhaust fan was blowing right into the tunnel.

They walked by lantern number one and were about halfway to number two when it happened. It was so sudden that Andrea didn't even realize what had taken place until it was too late. Not that she could have done anything about it anyway. The cool breeze suddenly became a powerful blast of cold air. It swooshed down the tunnel from the north, seeming to gather speed as it went. It extinguished all of the lamps in one long icy blast, leaving the two travellers completely and totally in the pitch black of the tunnel.

Andrea felt the frigid gust blow against her face. It sent Vance's cap hurtling off behind her and pulled at her old T-shirt. A loud, long piercing sound rent the air, vibrating down the tunnel. Once again a hand clamped itself over Andrea's mouth. At least this hand was clean, Andrea thought distractedly, clean and strong. The sound was quickly shut off and Andrea realized with a start that she must have screamed.

"Quiet, kid," a rough voice spoke in her ear. "We don't want the whole town to know that we're down here!" Andrea nodded and the hand slowly slipped from her face.

Andrea sagged against the dirt side of the tunnel, willing her jelly knees to work again. She still couldn't see a thing, but she knew Old Scarface was very near. She could hear his rapid breathing, feel his moist, cigar-tainted breath on her face. "Wind just blew out the lanterns, kid," Scarface explained, almost gently. "Happens all the time down here. You'll get used to it."

She heard the sound of a scrape and a flare of tiny light blinked into the darkness. Scarface had lit a match and was looking for the next lantern on the wall. He found it, lit it, then lit a cigar from the lantern flame. "Come on, girlie," he said, bending down to pick up her hat which had fallen at his feet, "let's get all these lanterns going again – no tellin' when we'll need 'em."

Scarface awkwardly set her cap back on her head. The brim hung over her eyes and she couldn't see. "G-Girlie?" she questioned shakily. How had he guessed? Hadn't she been careful enough?

He pulled the cap out of her eyes and set it more firmly on her short, spiky hair. "Yes, girlie," he repeated softly. He stuck his large stubby index finger into his ear and wiggled it. "Never heard a boy make a sound like that! Cleaned all the wax outta this ear, that's for sure. You got yourself a set of powerful lungs there. Ya might wanna look into singin' someday."

"O-oh!" Andrea shrank back against the wall even further. If it had been possible, she would have burrowed like a mole into the earth, never to be seen again. "Wha-what are you going to do to me?" She felt compelled to ask. The words just popped out of her mouth. She hated any kind of suspense.

"Do to you?" he chuckled and tapped her lightly on the cheek. See, he can be a nice man deep down, Andrea thought. She wondered for a brief moment just who she was trying to convince, but let the thought disappear in the semi-blackness of the tunnel. "You got it wrong, girlie."

"Wh-wha-what?" Andrea had to stop and clear her dry throat, forcing the word around a huge lump of fear that threatened to close off her windpipe.

"Look, I hired ya to do a job, right? Ya haven't done it yet!" Now he was starting to sound gruff and impatient again. "Just help me get these lanterns lit and get me to the Hazleton. I gotta keep a date with my best girl."

Andrea sagged once again against the tunnel wall, this time in relief. "Yes sir!" She would willingly help him light a million candles and lamps and get him to his destination too. She wondered again, though, about how unpredictable he was. If anything, she thought, he should be absolutely livid that she was female and had infiltrated his private underground man's world. This time she was thankful for his inconsistent character. Still, Andrea mused, it was almost as if he had two distinct personalities, one sort of nice and a little bit friendly, and the other mean and nasty and often dangerous. It was all so strange and unsettling. Nothing made sense down here in the underworld.

Andrea pushed all thoughts away for contemplation later and concentrated on the job at hand. "Ahead should be lantern number two," she muttered to herself as they walked slowly along.

"We need to get to number eight," Scarface added.

"How did you know that?" Andrea demanded. "I thought it was my job to help you find your way around down here!"

"Do ya think I'd trust the likes of you kids with my life?! Not a chance, girlie. That's why I'm the boss. That's why I've lived this long. I've kept a step ahead of the cops by usin' this," he pointed his cigar to his head. "I can outsmart anyone because I don't rely on anyone, see? I take care of Number One. You kids come in real handy, though, leadin' everyone else around. Ya run fast too, when ya need to."

That made sense to Andrea. She wouldn't be trusting anyone down here if she didn't have to, and unknowingly Ol' Scarface had helped her out. Eight. Lantern number eight. That's where Vance had said she would need to turn east again. The Hazleton was two lanterns along the second tunnel. They walked on slowly, side by side, feeling their way to the next lamp. Old Scarface's matches didn't last long, but the red glow from the end of his cigar helped to some extent, giving the tunnel a dull eerie glow.

Somewhere between the seventh and eighth lantern, Andrea came to a depression in the tunnel wall. She stopped and stretched her arm out further, trying to feel the solid dirt wall that she was used to touching. Nothing. "What's this?" she asked uncertainly. Scarface turned and shone his stogie in Andrea's direction. It gave enough light for them to distinguish a small hole; the kind made just for kids like her to crawl through.

"That leads right into the Hazleton, into the suite that I use when I'm here. Had it built 'specially for me, in the basement, near these escape tunnels. If you ever need to get to me quickly, that's where you come, hear?" He warned Andrea with a tilt of his head in her direction.

Andrea nodded and they continued down the narrow tunnel together. It seemed like an eternity, but they finally found the eighth lantern. Scarface carefully lit it and turned to take a good look at Andrea in the round yellow glow of light. "Ya got spunk, girlie", he declared. "I like that. And I like you." He turned east into the adjacent tunnel. The lanterns in this tunnel hadn't blown out and the rest of their journey to the Hazleton was swift and relatively easy. At the second lantern, Old Scarface took a coin out of his pocket and as usual flipped it in the air in her direction. Andrea managed to catch it single-handed.

"Thank you," she said solemnly, not sure whether she wanted compliments from a powerful and dangerous man like him.

"I got respect for people with courage," he continued, "and you got it. Even went through that small tunnel to do your job; warned my friends. I like you, girlie." He reached into his pocket again and brought out a few more coins.

"Thank you, Scar – ah – Mister –" Andrea stuttered. She didn't want to call him Scarface to his face, even though she was sure he knew that he had that nickname. It seemed disrespectful, somehow.

"Just call me Big Al," he said, reaching for her hand and dropping four more coins into her cold fingers. "I could use a spunky kid like you in my organization. We'd be good together – you 'n' me. Ya got guts, girlie." He tweaked her cheek once, then turned and tapped a coded knock on the invisible door. It opened in a flash and he stepped through into the lighted area. "What's your name?" he asked over his shoulder. "I always like to know the names of my friends."

Friends?! Andrea thought. Were they friends? She didn't think so, but she stammered out her name anyway. "An-Andy."

"Your real name, kid," he demanded, scowling back over his shoulder. He was losing his patience again.

"Oh, An-An-Andrea."

"See ya round, Andrea, and think about what I said. You could go far in my organization; be the top runner down here," he called over his shoulder. "What d'ya say?" He didn't wait for her to answer. "We'll talk about the job later. And don't worry, none, little Andrea, your secret's safe with me!" She thought she saw him wink once just as the door shut – but she wasn't sure.

10:00 PM Friday Night

DECISIONS, DECISIONS

A ndrea sank against the wall of the tunnel, deciding
that she deserved a break after all that excitement.
She sure didn't understand Ol' Scarface at all! One
minute he seemed ready to hit her for bursting through
the door without knocking; the next minute he was
almost caressing her cheek and calling her "girlie,"
telling her they'd make a good team and practically
demanding that she call him Big Al, as if they were the
best of friends. It felt good to be appreciated, but could
Andrea really trust Scarface/Big Al? Whatever she
called him, he still seemed to be a person best avoided.

It was nice to think that somebody thought she
could do a good job, though. Just think, she could be

the number one tunnel runner. The personal helper to Big Al. She would get all of the best trips and personally escort Big Al wherever he wanted to go. She'd meet all sorts of interesting people. And make some money besides. What prestige! She smiled to herself and straightened her shoulders. Maybe she could just live with Big Al or Rosie. How exciting that would be! They both seemed to like her. And as she got to know Big Al, he'd really grow to like her and he wouldn't lose his temper at her. Maybe she could even help Vance too by asking Big Al to quit picking on him. The thought appealed greatly to Andrea. She liked to see herself as a protector. Vance would be happy that she – Andrea caught her breath and shivered. She suddenly realized that Big Al was basically offering her Vance's job!

She leaned heavily against the tunnel wall again, feeling like a low-down, double-crossing friend. She couldn't take Vance's job. That would be wrong. Why would Big Al have offered it to her? Andrea was truly puzzled – unless he intended to give Vance some kind of promotion. That was it. She would get Vance's job because he was moving on to bigger and better things inside the organization. That had to be it! Oh, she just couldn't wait to tell her grandfather. He would be so proud of her!

Andrea felt the happy feeling disappear as sadness flooded her being. She had been so busy trying to fit into this time period; she had had so many adventures that she hadn't even had time to think much about her family or herself. Where were they and what were they doing? Were they all at the restaurant, frantically searching for her?

More importantly at the moment, Andrea wondered where would she go tonight when this job was done. Where would she sleep? Where would she live? A desolate feeling of loneliness crept into her heart. She supposed she could become a street person and live in a park somewhere. Did they even have street people in the 1920s, she wondered. At least it was summer and she could do that for a few months until it grew cold outside. Then she would have to make other arrangements. She could probably find a hole in the tunnels and call that home, she thought, shuddering at the idea. The tunnels really gave her the creeps and she couldn't imagine actually living in one. Tears began to form in her eyes as Andrea thought about never seeing her family again. Blinking rapidly to stem the flow, she took a huge calming breath and exhaled slowly. Maybe Vance would have some idea about where she could live. That thought buoyed her spirits and she set off in search of Vance. She would ask him the first chance she got.

Andrea scurried along in the tunnel she nicknamed Windy, constantly in fear that the strange wind might blow suddenly and choke out all of the lanterns again. She didn't have matches and sure didn't want to be alone in the total darkness if that should happen again. She could feel the slight cool breeze in the tunnel. It made a soft moaning sound, causing the hairs on her arms to stand up. Her neck felt suddenly chilled. It reminded her of the long corridors at school. There was often a blast of air that rushed from one hallway to another. It had something to do with air pressure, she remembered, and it could become quite drafty under the right conditions. Andrea supposed that that was the same thing that happened in the tunnels, although it seemed much more spooky and ghost-like down here.

She trampled on something that made a rustling sound beneath her feet and stopped short in fear. What could it be? Nervously, she bent over and peered at the ground. In the dim yellow light she could see something crumpled up, lying in the gravel and dirt in front of her. A newspaper! It must have blown in when the huge gust of air had extinguished the lights. Andrea picked it up and smoothed it out. She walked to the nearest lantern and held the news-paper up to catch the weak rays of light. Her hands trembled slightly when she found what she was look-ing for – the date. "July 5, 1924," she read slowly.

Andrea stared at it for several seconds, hoping to see the numbers magically change, but they didn't. Unfortunately, the paper looked in good condition, except for having been crumpled, so it couldn't have been very old. It didn't have that yellow aged look she had seen on some of the mementos and clippings her grandparents kept in a special photo album. This was more concrete evidence that she had somehow gone back in time. Andrea grimly folded the newspaper and stuck it in the back pocket of her overalls. She would read it later. Maybe it would give her some clues on how to survive in this out-dated world. With a sigh of resignation, Andrea pushed on in search of Vance.

She quickly found herself back at the tunnel that led under Main Street. Andrea turned into it and half ran to get back to the more familiar tunnels near Scotty's. She had no plan except to try to find Vance. She knew that she would eventually find him near The Four Star Café or the train station, so she headed in that direction, the coins in her pocket making a jingling sound as she ran.

She had – Andrea stopped for a moment near the next lantern and pulled the coins out of her pocket, quickly counting – seven coins. That was probably a lot of money for this time period. She wondered what she could buy with them. She wondered too if they were worth anything in modern times. She slid the coins back into her pocket as she came to the entrance of the other tunnel and turned south. The weight of the coins reassured her. It felt good to have them there, although she wasn't sure what she would do with them.

The sound of running footsteps caught her attention. They were coming from behind her. Friend or foe, Andrea wondered, trying to decide whether or not she should find a place to hide. There must be other kids doing this job, Andrea thought, although she had only seen Vance so far. How would they feel about having other people infringe on their territory and their money-making potential?

They wouldn't like it much, Andrea decided, remembering how angry Vance had gotten after their first trip. He sure didn't like to share, and Andrea couldn't blame him. This could be very dangerous work and he probably did need the money. And it was an adventure, Andrea had to admit, working for bad guys and running around all night long. Andrea wondered what Vance's family was like. Why would his parents let him do this kind of work? They must realize how dangerous it was.

Andrea had just decided to hide in some small crack in the tunnel wall and let the other person pass by, when she heard her name being called faintly in the tunnel.

"Andy." It echoed with a supernatural quality that caused Andrea to jump. It must be Vance, she thought. No one else knew her name except Ol' Scarface, and he probably couldn't run that fast. She stepped into the centre of the tunnel near a lantern and let Vance catch up. He was in a hurry, Andrea decided, watching him run pell-mell down the tunnel.

"What's your big hurry?" she demanded as he skidded to a stop only centimetres from her outstretched arms. She was sure that he would run into her and was trying to protect herself.

"We got another job," Vance puffed. He grabbed her arm. "Come on," he panted. "More fellas to pick up at the train."

"How do you know?" Andrea asked.

"I told ya, I got inside connections! We usually get our orders from the Station or The Four Star, remember. This one came down from somewhere else. Don't worry about it. It's from a reliable source."

Since Andrea had nothing else to do, she sprinted after Vance, letting him lead the way back to the train station. He veered around the centre pole that marked the café entrance and waved exuberantly at it, reminding Andrea to watch herself. She could see that it would be easy to run into it. The pole barely showed up at all in the shadowed light.

Andrea skirted the pole and jogged on, following Vance. She felt confident enough to relax a bit. Let him be in charge for a while, she thought. I need a mental break from all this stress.

A few minutes later, they again entered into the tiny caretaker's room at the train station. This time Andrea was prepared for the cramped conditions and didn't even mind the smell of the cleaning fluids.

Light seeped in under the door. Their eyes adjusted

very quickly and Andrea saw that Vance had squatted against the wall between the mops and brooms. "Take a break," he told her. "We've got a few minutes before the train gets in. This one's usually late."

Andrea joined him on the floor, sitting tailor style, squashed between the wall and the large drum. "What do you think is in here?" she asked tapping it softly with her fingernail.

Vance shrugged, uninterested. "Cleaning stuff, I guess."

It was the first time all evening that she had sat and it felt good to rest her feet. "You tell Rosie to go the Hazleton?" Andrea asked to make conversation. It felt funny to be sitting in such intimate circumstances with a person of the opposite sex. She felt uncomfortable. Andrea always chatted when she felt that way.

"Yeah," Vance answered. "Got a nice couple a coins for my trouble too."

More silence. What kind of conversation did you have with a boy, Andrea wondered. She didn't have that much experience with boys in the modern world, so how on earth could she know what to talk about in this strange era? "Have you got a family?" Andrea suddenly burst out. The words bounced off the metal of the buckets and pails sounding tinny to her ears.

"A family?!" Vance asked disbelieving, and Andrea knew with a sinking feeling that she'd made a big mistake. Obviously a boy in the 1920s didn't talk about families. That probably made him feel like a sissy.

"You know," Andrea continued bravely. "Brothers, sisters, mother, father – that sort of thing."

Vance snorted in disgust. "Yeah, I got a family. What d'ya think I'm doing this for? I got a young sister – just a kid, and my ma. She's sick, though; she's tired all the time. Got no pa," he thumped on the floor in disgust. "Left long ago. Don't even know if I'd recognize him if I saw him. Good fer nuthin'...." Vance let the thought die.

"What about you?" he asked a few moments later, now feeling obligated to carry on a conversation. "You must be new in town. I ain't never seen you around before."

"Yeah, I'm new," Andrea quickly agreed. What could she say? That she was from the future, and hoped like anything to be going back there soon? Could she talk about her "normal" family with a mother who drove cars? A father who loved to cook and clean house and her bratty brother, Tony? Could she talk about video games and the latest computer technology? What about cell phones and even television? What could she say?!

"H-how's your eye?" Andrea suddenly remembered.

"Fine," Vance practically barked. "If I don't think about it," he added more quietly.

"You really should be more careful," Andrea admonished.

"Careful?!" Vance practically spat the word into her face.

"Yeah, that pole is dangerous." Andrea felt her heart pounding in her chest. Suddenly it was very important for her to believe that Ol' Scarface wasn't so nasty. She didn't want to believe that he was violent and hurtful. She just couldn't face the truth. She came from a world where the adults she knew were loving and kind.

The silence in the tiny room was deafening as Vance regarded Andrea with disbelieving eyes. "Ya know this shiner is thanks to Ol' Scarface," he said bluntly. "Why would ya pretend differently?"

"No!" Andrea denied, refusing to take in the evidence presented right in front of her. "He wouldn't do that –"

Vance snorted. "And what about what he done to ya – pullin' yer hair and makin' ya go in that tiny tunnel?"

Andrea felt her face grow hot and wondered briefly why she thought she needed to protect the man. "H-he was just worried about his friends, that's all," she muttered weakly. It sounded lame even to her own ears.

"Sheesh!" Vance scratched his head, bewildered. "Yer pullin' the wool over yer own eyes, Andy! Be careful with him. He's not to be trusted."

"But he can be nice –" Vance snorted again. "At least sometimes," she conceded.

"Get yer head outta the sand, boy! Who are ya

tryin' ta kid? Scarface ain't no saint. He'd probably kill his own mother, if he thought he had cause, and never think about it again. That's the kinda man he is."

"I-I don't believe it." Andrea retorted stubbornly. "He's not that bad!"

"Better watch yerself, Andy," Vance sneered. "He's really got you fooled." She watched in the dim light of the small room as Vance's good eye narrowed into a slit as an idea suddenly occurred. "I'll just bet ya he's gone an' offered ya my job too! Hasn't he?"

Andrea's guilty start gave Vance the only reply he needed. "What a –" The rest of Vance's angry retort was lost in the long toot of the train whistle as it sounded in the distance. Vance got abruptly to his feet. "I suppose yer gonna double-cross me too," he muttered sadly, his back to Andrea.

"No, Vance, I would never do that," she lied. She had been considering doing just that by accepting the job, hadn't she? Or did she really, honestly believe that Ol' Scarface would find another job for Vance; a better job?

Vance heaved a big sigh, his shoulders hunching. "I'm gonna trust ya, Andy." He spoke softly, still facing the door. "I always try ta trust a person and hope that if I show trust, he'll return the favour. My ma taught me that." Vance seemed to visibly push aside his worries as he straightened his body. "You remember ta stay quiet in here and wait for me, hear?"

"Yeah, I hear ya," came Andrea's soft reply. As Vance slipped out of the room and quickly closed the door, Andrea felt an enormous burden of guilt and sadness weigh heavily on her shoulders. It hurt to admit that she wasn't sure she deserved Vance's trust at the moment.

10:15 PM Friday night

WORRIES AND INTERRUPTIONS

Andrea was never sure how long it took Vance to return. It could have been hours, although she was pretty sure that it was only a matter of minutes. She listened to the loud rumble of the train as it pulled into the station. She heard the hiss of the brakes first being applied and then being released. She heard the movement of people on the stairs outside her door and wondered at the number of passengers disembarking at Moose Jaw. It sounded like a huge crowd.

Andrea concentrated on not thinking about Vance and Big Al and trust. She was totally bewildered by her reactions to the man. Why would she even want to befriend a criminal, or have one befriend her?! Her parents would never condone such behavior. Purposefully, Andrea let her mind go blank, refusing to let herself think of anything.

She felt safe and secure in the small room and fell into a warm stupor as she waited for Vance. She had been tired from the drive to Moose Jaw earlier in the day. Was that only this afternoon? Andrea reflected; it seemed like another lifetime. Indeed, it was another lifetime. Would she ever see her family again? she wondered. A small lonely ache crept into the region of her heart and tears smarted in her eyes. How would she ever get home?

Sudden footsteps interrupted her thoughts and Andrea quickly forgot about being lonely. The footsteps sounded different, louder somehow, as if a heavier person was walking straight toward her door! It can't be, she thought. No one would come in here except for the caretaker, and hopefully he was busy elsewhere.

Andrea held her breath, waiting for the footsteps to turn and march up the stairs and into the train station like all of the rest had done. But they didn't. They hesitated near the door, as if the person was looking around. Someone's coming in here! Andrea's mind fairly screamed with fright. What should she do? The footfalls stopped right outside the door and Andrea scooted around to hide behind the huge drum of cleaning solution. She thought about diving back into the tunnel to hide, but it was too late. She was stuck. In her stupor, she had waited too long to react and was now going to be caught! Andrea slid backward on her buttocks until her back touched the wall. Then she scrunched her body up as small as she could. She sure didn't want to get caught here. If she did, she supposed she could always pretend that she needed a place to sleep, which she did.

Andrea stayed put, making sure that the mops and brooms leaning against the wall would shield her from view. She drew her knees up to her chest and wrapped her arms around them to keep them from shaking. She rested her chin on the dusty jeans material against her legs and willed her trembling body to be calm.

She had barely gotten settled when the door creaked open. Andrea saw a pair of shiny black boots move quickly into the room. As the door swung shut, the light reflected off two rows of shiny buttons marching down the front of a dark-coloured jacket. It looked like a uniform, a policeman's uniform. The boots looked like the ones she had gotten a brief glimpse of through the hole when she was hiding at Scotty's. Was it a policeman? She wondered what he wanted.

Andrea didn't have to wait long to find out. Only moments later the door opened again. Another body squashed its way into the already crowded room and quickly closed the door. "Anyone see you?" a raspy voice asked.

"Don't think so," the second voice replied. "I was careful."

"You said you had information."

"I do." The second voice suddenly sounded cocky and confident.

"Well, spill it, man!" The first voice demanded.

"What's in it for me?" the cocky voice wanted to know. "I'm riskin' my life informin' like this – could get m'self killed."

"You're wasting my time!" The voice of the police officer sounded even raspier.

"Then I'll just keep my information to myself." The door suddenly opened for a brief second. It was slammed shut just as quickly, but not before Andrea got a glimpse of the two men crowding the tiny room. One was indeed wearing a policeman's uniform and the other was a scrawny guy she was sure she'd seen before.

"Okay. Okay," the cop relented. There was the sound of crumpling paper. "Here's some dough."

"How much?" the scrawny informer wanted to know.

"Enough! And if your information turns out to be good, I'll see that you get more."

"Now yer talkin'." Andrea was sure that she recognized the voice, but who was it, and what was he going to say? In the pit of her stomach, a cold feeling burst forth and began to spread. It was about Big Al, she was sure. And the scrawny guy was – was – why, of course! This scrawny informant was Joe, from Scotty's Shoe Store, the guy who had told her to be sure and let Big Al know that Rosie wanted to see him at the Hazleton. It must have been a set- up. No wonder Joe had looked so cagey then. What a snitch!

"He's in town tonight," Joe broke into Andrea's thoughts.

"Who?" the cop demanded.

"Old Scarface, that's who. He's at the Hazleton Hotel right this very minute. You can catch him if you get there quick."

"How do you know this?" the cop wanted to know.

"I have my own sources," Joe replied smugly. "You just go and do your job so that I can get what's comin' to me."

A match was suddenly lit in the room. Andrea shrank back against the wall holding her breath. She saw the uniformed man pull a watch out of his pocket and study its face. "It's 10:30," he reported. "I'll need to round up some reinforcements. They're all out on patrol now. In an hour," he decided. "At 11:30 we'll raid the Hazleton, not a moment sooner, got that?" The match burned down and was blown out.

"Why should I care?" Joe retorted. "I've done my bit, the rest is up to you."

"Yes it is," the cop agreed. "But I don't want anything to go wrong tonight! I've been chasing this guy for a long time, and he always manages to escape. I want him. You don't breathe a word of this plan to anyone, and if you happen to see him and he's not at the Hazleton, you let me know."

"Sure thing." The rat Joe agreed too readily. Andrea was sure that he would just take his money and run in the other direction.

"Now tell me, what's happening at Scotty's Shoe Store?" the officer suddenly changed the subject.

The question obviously took Joe by surprise, because he coughed and sputtered a few times before finally finding his voice. "What do ya mean?" he croaked hoarsely. "Nothin's going on at Scotty's. I was just visiting my buddy."

"Sure, sure," the policeman agreed sarcastically. "And my mother's Lady Godiva."

"That I'd like to see," Joe asserted.

"Never you mind!" the cop snarled. "We're not finished about Scotty's, but I've got to get this next plan under way. We'll talk about Scotty's again," he threatened. "And next time you *will* talk!"

Andrea listened, fascinated. She thought for sure that Joe would give everything away for a price. She wondered what made him so secretive about Scotty's, and yet so willing to rat on Big Al. Maybe there was some sort of loyalty in this underground world after all, since Joe was obviously trying to protect Scotty.

Andrea had noticed for some time that her left foot

was falling asleep. The circulation had been cut off and pins and needles began to prick the sole. The pain and ticklishness of it was almost unbearable. She moved slightly to try to relieve the pressure and accidentally knocked a galvanised bucket. It clattered loudly in the darkness. "What was that?!" The wiry informant demanded.

"Just a rat," the cop replied, unconcerned. Just like you, Joe. The unspoken words hung in the air. They were so tangible that Andrea was sure she could read them in the lightless room.

"Look, you wanted information," Joe tried to justify. "I'm just doing my duty!"

"Yeah, sure." The cop pushed the smaller man aside almost roughly and opened the caretaker's door. "I'm just doing my duty too," he replied, shaking his head. "But you kind of have to admire the man. Ol' Scarface is as sly as a fox and weasly as a weasel. Why, he's no different than a lot of folks who live around here, is he? You sure have to wonder about some of Moose Jaw's 'fine, upstanding citizens,' with all the things that go on around here." He sternly pointed his finger at the other man, changing the subject. "Remember, not one word to anyone." With that he disappeared out of the door.

"And who would I tell?" Joe whispered into the darkness of the caretaker's room. "The rat in the corner?"

Andrea almost jumped. He was talking about her!

But he didn't know she was there, did he? She forgot to breathe. Her heart pounded in her chest so loudly that Andrea was sure it could be heard for miles around. She closed her eyes and wished herself a million miles away from this place; she longed to be anywhere but here.

Joe nervously lit a match and held it aloft. It gave off faint light. Andrea buried her head on her knees, pulling herself back further against the wall, willing herself to become invisible. If she could have, she would have turned into a ghost, totally invisible to the naked eye. She held her breath, squeezed her eyes shut, and tried to disappear. A sudden scurrying of tiny feet was heard in the opposite corner of the room. Joe turned his back on Andrea and shuffled closer to investigate.

The match burned down. The man uttered a soft curse and loudly sucked his fingers in the dark. "Just me and the rats, huh?" he muttered. He stood stiff and quiet for a long moment, listening, Andrea assumed, for another sound that would give her away. She still held her breath, not daring to breathe, her lungs bursting for air. Joe finally shuffled the few steps to the door and opened it, disappearing into the bright light of the hallway, stealthily closing the door behind him.

Andrea did not move for a few minutes, petrified that he might be waiting and listening just outside the door. She did allow herself to breathe, though, in tiny silent gulps that were hard to control. Her mind raced, wondering what to do with the information she had just heard. Vance had said to wait right here, but Big Al was in trouble! Andrea felt as if she was being torn in two. She owed Ol' Scarface her loyalty and help, didn't she? After all, he had been a friend to her, no matter what Vance thought. He hadn't gotten angry, even when she'd screamed so loudly in his ear. And yet he was a criminal and he had hurt both her and Vance. On top of everything else, he was willing to throw Vance over, making Andrea his new best tunnel boy.

Oh, what to do?! Nothing was clear anymore. Doing right and wrong seemed all mixed up in her mind. Should she wait for Vance, or run and let Big Al know that there was about to be a raid and he was the number one target? Or should she just pretend that she had never overheard that particular conversation and let him get captured? These thoughts and many more bombarded her brain, giving Andrea a sudden and intense headache.

Suddenly Andrea heard the clatter of shoes running on the stairs and heard the thump of the door. Vance came flying in, almost slamming the door behind him. "Andy?"

"Right here, Vance," she answered in relief. She wanted to throw her arms around him for the second time that night. He had come back for her. Good old trustworthy Vance. "I've –"

"Ya got a trip," Vance interrupted hurriedly. "Two guys who want to go the Imperial."

"The Imperial?"

"Imperial Hotel," he replied impatiently.

"But Vance, I don't know where that is," she uttered tiredly. Suddenly this dangerous game was too much for her. Andrea wanted out. She just wanted to go home; to be back with her family celebrating Vanessa's wedding. Even being a junior bridesmaid seemed suddenly a million times more agreeable than playing life and death games with criminals in underground Moose Jaw.

Vance noted the change in her voice. He must have heard the exhaustion, for he explained, almost gently, "It's three lamps over to the café and then seven lamps west, Andy. The night's just about over. We don't usually get much action after midnight, so you can go home soon."

Home. It sounded so wonderful, Andrea thought. But would she ever see her home again? "Why the Imperial Hotel?" she asked irritably. "Why not just the Hazleton? I know where that hotel is!"

"The Imperial Hotel has Turkish baths. Lots of fellas enjoy that along with their liquor. Anyway, get movin' on this one, Andy, and then you can go home."

Tears gathered in Andrea's eyes. "I-I ain't got no home," she told Vance tearily, slipping unconsciously into the slang of the underground. "I don't know where home is right now."

He was silent for a moment, as if making a decision. He placed a comforting arm around Andrea's trembling shoulders. "You can come home with me," he invited quietly. "Ma won't mind. We got enough to eat – 'specially with the money I made tonight." He rattled the coins in his pocket.

"Even after…." Andrea whispered. She let the thought die on nerveless lips.

"Yeah," Vance agreed awkwardly, "even after that. Friends come first in my book."

Andrea was so relieved she felt tears flood into her eyes. Then she remembered her coins. Andrea reached into her pocket with trembling fingers and pulled out the loot. "Here, Vance," she whispered, placing the coins into his warm firm hand. "You take this for my room and board. I don't need it."

"Not this much, Andy," Vance protested weakly. He looked as though he held a king's ransom in his outstretched hand. "Though we really could use the dough." This was spoken so softly that Andrea had to strain to hear the words.

"You take care of it, Vance," she told him, seeing him waver. She wanted to save his pride. He had been nice to her and she wanted to repay him for his kindness. "We'll discuss it later." Andrea spoke in a firm voice. "Right now I have a job to do, and so do you."

"Right." Vance smoothly pocketed the money. That action. There it was again; that feeling of having seen someone do that exact same thing a hundred times before.

Even in the darkness of the room, she knew what he was doing. She could see it in her memory, even though she couldn't put a face to the other person whose actions she knew so well.

"You take those guys ta the Imperial. I'll take my trip to Scotty's and on further to a top secret place and meet ya back at The Four Star Café, okay?"

"Sure," Andrea agreed quietly. She let her moment of déjà vu slip away. One last trip. It shouldn't be that difficult. "Where do I meet the men?"

"On the train platform, just like before. My errand starts here, so I'll just leave now. See ya soon, Andy," Vance called over his shoulder. He slid behind the mops and brooms and disappeared into the tunnel.

"Vance, wait!" Andrea suddenly remembered that she hadn't told him about the plan to capture Big Al tonight. But Vance was gone. He had disappeared into the tunnels faster than a hunted rodent. Oh, what was she going to do? Now Andrea would have to act on her own. She hadn't had time to ask Vance for his advice on what she should do. What time was it? Did she have time to take the men to the Imperial and then warn Big Al at the Hazleton? Did she really want to? And what about Joe? Did she need to consider his safety in all of this?

Andrea wondered just where her own loyalties should lie. With her new friend, Vance, who was willing to give her shelter even though she might double-cross him and steal his job? Or with Ol' Scarface, alias Big Al, who seemed to have befuddled her with all his talk of being a team and leading an exciting life in the tunnels? Perhaps staying underground in this surreal world made a person question right and wrong.

Also weighing heavily on Andrea's mind was the thought of not helping Big Al and then being found out. Even the slim chance of having to endure his wrath yet again left Andrea trembling in fear. Andrea wondered how her parents would handle something like this. She suddenly wished she could talk to them. They would know what to do, and they would sure like Vance, she decided. Vance seemed to know the right thing to do, even though it would hurt him in the end. He really knew what friendship and loyalty was all about. Maybe Andrea had a few lessons to learn about being a good friend. She definitely had a lot of thinking to do, but first of all, she had one last trip to take. Would she have time to think and come to a decision while she made that trip? She hoped so, because that was her plan. She didn't know what else to do.

10:40 PM Friday Night

THE CATASTROPHE

Andrea found the two men waiting for her on the train platform, just as Vance has indicated. One was very tall and thin, with a black moustache. The other was probably of average height with a more stocky build. Andrea figured that he looked so short and chubby because he stood beside such a tall skinny person. My last trip, Andrea thought with relief and regret. It had been fun in a weird sort of way.

She gave a slight nod of her head and the men fell into step behind her, following her down into the underpass and into the small cleaning room. It was so easy now, this voyaging underground like a nocturnal animal, so simple that Andrea could almost have done it in her sleep. It could have been fun, if it wasn't so dangerous. A little excitement in your life was great, Andrea thought, but the hazards of the job – of getting into someone's bad books, as she had done with Old Scarface, of getting caught – that was another thing. Andrea knew that some of the men, if not all of them, carried guns. She had seen the bulges in their jackets and this worried her. You never knew when some guy might take out his gun and just start shooting.

The men followed silently behind Andrea as they journeyed toward the Imperial. Andrea wondered what Turkish baths were. She had heard the expression before, but didn't know exactly what it meant. Perhaps it had something to do with the naturally hot mineral water that had been discovered near Moose Jaw. The water was warmed inside the earth and came to the surface still very hot. People claimed that it cured all sorts of ailments. Andrea was somewhat skeptical about that, but she had bathed in the waters at the new spa that had opened near Crescent Park, enjoying the warm relaxed feeling it gave her.

The small party turned west at the third lantern, and Andrea heard one of the men whisper. It sounded like: "Pst…pst…pst…Scarface…." A picture of Big Al popped into her mind. How could she have forgotten?! What was she to do? To rescue Big Al or not, that was the question.

Could she actually do it? Did she have time to get the men to the Imperial and then run like a speed demon through the tunnels over to the Hazleton? The hotels were practically at opposite ends of town from one another. They were as far apart as any of the underground places Andrea had visited so far. But, even more importantly, should she? Andrea was torn with indecision. Sure, Ol' Scarface had been nice to her, but he had also hurt her, and Vance too. And he carried a gun as well. Would he use it on her if he found out that she had had the chance to help him and didn't?

In her agitation and indecision, Andrea unknowingly picked up speed, travelling faster and faster through the tunnel. She felt like the race walkers she had seen on TV. It felt good to think of her own world and she let the feeling flow through her tired limbs. She could hear the two men behind her huffing as they hastened along. "What's your hurry, kid?" one of them finally called out as they neared the second lantern in the tunnel moving westward. "Slow down at bit, will ya?"

"Sorry," Andrea mumbled automatically. She wasn't really sorry at all – her only thoughts were of Big Al and whether or not she should try to rescue him by getting to the Hazleton before the police. Andrea did slow down a fraction, wondering if she had the right to ask the men to hurry up. She thought about telling them of her dilemma, but she didn't really trust them. It was hard to know who to trust in this crazy mixed-up world.

Andrea had just decided definitely not to spill the beans to the men when she heard an enormous boom.

It shook the tunnel, knocking the three travellers off their feet. A huge spray of dirt and dust roared through the tunnel with incredible force, causing the lantern nearest the party to sputter and die. "What was that?!" Andrea choked as she fell to her knees. Never in her life had she experienced anything like this, what could it be?!

"Must be a cave-in," one of the men replied, hacking on the dirt and dust.

"A cave-in?!" Andrea repeated, dumbfounded. She had never even considered the possibility! She had spent her time worrying about rats and rodents, spiders and police. In her naiveté, she had just assumed that the tunnels would be safe and well-built. After all, technology and safety regulations.... There she went again, thinking in terms of the future.

"Probably a new section of tunnel." Andrea could hear the men brushing the dirt from their clothes and hair. "Guess they didn't have a chance to make it real secure yet."

New section of tunnel? Andrea hadn't thought much about the tunnels. She had foolishly taken for granted their sturdiness and their presence. Who had built them? Were they continuing to build them now? How could they have done it so secretively, that even the policemen in town didn't know of their existence? Andrea had no answers; just more and more questions that filled her mind.

They waited for several moments while the dust settled, then ventured forth cautiously, creeping along with every step in the pitch dark. "Go back and grab that lighted lantern from the pole, way back there," the shorter man ordered. "We can't see a blinking thing in here." He seemed to naturally take charge, for the lanky guy meekly did as he was bid, returning quickly with the light. He held it aloft so that it shone into the darkness ahead.

Andrea was afraid to go on. "C-can't it happen again?" she asked worriedly.

"I suppose so," one of the men agreed, "but we need to go and investigate. Someone could be hurt." They continued cautiously, the lanky man holding the lantern above their heads as they crept on.

They came at last to a pile of dirt and debris blocking the tunnel. It looked as if the wall of the tunnel had given in. The dirt and large timbers, obviously used to help support the weight, lay in a tangled mess on the tunnel floor. "It's not too bad," the shorter man assessed. Andrea found herself giving him the nickname Chubs. "There's a small space there," he pointed to a tiny space between the dirt ceiling and the pile of debris. "Someone could crawl through to see what the other side looks like." He looked straight at Andrea.

Andrea studied the small space. She knew just which someone they had in mind. Only she would fit! That's one of the reasons they use kids for this job, she suddenly realized. Their small bodies could squeeze into odd and small places, and besides, one dead kid or two probably didn't make a difference to anyone. There was no way they would get her into that tiny space, she determined. She could just barely see the light seeping in from the other side. Chubs kicked at the pile of rubble with his boot. "Not enough mess for anyone to be caught under it," he guessed. "We'd see an arm or leg, or something."

Chubs climbed the pile of dirt and was peering over it to the other side. "I think there's enough room for one of us to climb through," he repeated. "The cave-in was small, just in this little area. I can see that it's clear on the other side. Help me clear some of the boards and dirt away."

Stilts, as Andrea nicknamed the other man, joined Chubs on the heap of earth and they began to heave the large planks of wood out of the way. There were only two or three of them as far as Andrea could tell, but they were buried in the debris. They had to use their hands to scoop the dirt away in order to free the boards so that they could be removed.

Andrea watched as the men worked, a plan forming in her overanxious brain. There was no way that she was going to crawl into the unknown like that! She had done her bit going through that small dirt hole to warn the people at Scotty's. Once a night – once in a lifetime – was enough! There was no telling what was on the other side, and she wasn't about to find out. But she also knew what would happen if she refused to help these men. They would not take no for an answer and she would be in physical danger if she stayed....

A plan of sorts sprang into her mind as Andrea watched the men heave another huge piece of lumber toward the dirt wall. It landed with a muted thud which seemed to jar her brain into action. Since she refused to crawl through the tiny space, she would need to make a fast retreat. She would sneak away and head over to the Hazleton Hotel as fast as she could. She prayed that she would be in time to save Big Al. That way, if Stilts or Chubs ever squealed on her, she would have a good excuse. She would be able to say, in all honesty, that she had suddenly remembered the time and left on the double to reach Ol' Scarface in time. Surely he would believe that. After all, he would probably think it was more important to save his own skin than to rescue these two clowns.

Andrea hoped that it would never come to that. She knew that Big Al would be very angry that she hadn't come to save him first and he would want to know why. She wouldn't be able to tell him the truth; that she had been debating, wrestling with her conscience; that she wasn't sure that she wanted to rescue him in the first place.

It was a shaky, flimsy plan, but it was all Andrea could come up with under such stressful circumstances. I am

just a kid, she reminded herself with chagrin. A kid, playing a dangerous adult game and trying to survive.

Little sparks of hesitation pricked at her conscience, but Andrea firmly closed her mind to
thoughts of black and white and good and evil. She
was going to rescue Big Al, if she could get there in
time; it was the only way she could think of to save
her own skin. She took a quiet step back. Intuition
told her that the men would not be too happy to have
her run away. Luckily, the two of them were so busy
they didn't even notice her retreat. She took another
silent step back and then another and still another,
until the men began to fade away in the distance. She
walked backward step by step until she could just
barely hear the men's voices as they worked, then she
turned and ran like the wind.

"Hey! Where's the kid?" She heard the shout and
hurried even faster down the tunnel toward The Four
Star Café. She heard scraping and scurrying noises in
the distance and wondered if the men would try to follow her. It didn't matter. She had quite a head start on
them. She ran faster and faster, all her thoughts pinned
on getting to the Hazleton before the raid took place.

ANDREA REACHED THE MAIN TUNNEL that led along
Main Street and turned north into it. She was breathing heavily now and almost didn't see the centre pole

marking the entrance to the Café. At the last moment she swerved, narrowly avoiding it. A collision with that pole would be disastrous.

Andrea's chest hurt. She slowed for a moment, gulping the putrid tunnel air.

I've got to go on, she kept telling herself. Now that I've decided to do this, I've got to get there in time!

Taking two more gasps of stale air, Andrea forced herself to run on. She flew down the centre of the tunnel as fast as her weary, trembling legs would carry her, reaching the tunnel under Main Street in record time. Rest, Andrea thought, her heart pounding in her chest. She felt light-headed and leaned against the entrance. There she paused for a moment until her breathing slowed and her legs felt less rubbery. I'm going to make it, she repeated again and again. I *have* to make it in time!

Andrea pushed away from the wall, almost jumping into the tunnel. She'd forgotten about its being less tall than the other tunnels and brushed her hat on the dirt roof. When it fell off behind her, Andrea didn't even stop to pick it up. She barely noticed that it was gone.

It was a relatively short distance under Main Street, and then Andrea turned north into the last tunnel. Eight lanterns, she remembered. Eight lanterns until the hidden entrance to the Hazleton.

Andrea ran on, adrenalin giving her energy. She counted the lanterns out loud as she ran by each one.

Between six and seven, Andrea suddenly screeched to a halt, staring at the small freshly-dug hole. What had Big Al said about it? "If you ever need to get a holda me quickly, that's where you come, hear?" His words swooped into her mind. Andrea didn't even stop to think about what she was doing. She dropped to her hands and knees and crawled as fast as possible to get there in time.

This minuscule tunnel was even worse than the other. It was smaller and felt more claustrophobic. It smelled dank and moist, as if water was seeping in from somewhere. The thought of another cave-in filled her mind, threatening to send her into a state of panic. Come on, Andrea willed, pushing her body to the limit of its endurance. She had to make it, not only did Big Al's safety depend on it, but so did hers! She willed her mind totally blank, concentrating only on getting to the Hazleton in time.

Andrea pushed on in complete darkness for what seemed like ages. Then her mission was over. There was her goal! Directly ahead she spied light seeping through the void. It was another vent in the wall, just like the one at Scotty's. Not waiting to knock politely on the wall or to call out courteously, Andrea crawled directly to the vent and pushed with all her might.

The vent gave way and Andrea tumbled head first into the room. For the second time that night, she interrupted Old Scarface. She landed with a resounding bang that startled both Big Al and Rosie. They jumped from their positions, startled by the sudden intrusion. They had been sitting close together on the couch.

"What's going on?" Big Al demanded, jumping to his feet, instinctively reaching for the gun holster strapped to his side. Rosie sat clutching her feather boa around her shoulders.

"No time to explain!" Andrea burst out, gasping for air. "You've got to get out of here now! The cops are coming!"

Big Al looked as if he was going to argue with Andrea for a moment. Then he took a look at her dishevelled appearance, her filthy face, and the stricken look in her eyes and took her at her word. "All right, kid, let's go."

Rosie quickly gathered up her few belongings and headed for the secret passageway hidden behind another armoire. It was almost identical to the one at the Café. It was a good thing the cupboards were so popular and so large, Andrea thought. If the cops were smart, they would soon put two and two together and begin to wonder about the huge wooden cupboards at Scotty's, in the Hazleton, and at The Four Star Café.

It was Big Al who swept up the dirt this time and hurriedly replaced the vent. He put the dirt into the fireplace where a cozy fire warmed the basement room. "Can't make it too easy for 'em," he muttered under his breath as he quickly scattered the burning embers throughout the fireplace. Andrea realized that he was trying to make it look as if the fire had been burning for a long time and was nearly out. "That'll do," he said, taking a look around to make sure that no personal belongings or damning evidence would be left behind.

Big Al grabbed his jacket and flung it over his shoulder, motioning to Andrea from across the room. He pulled at the armoire. It was hinged to a hidden door in the wall, which, when opened, revealed a large hiding space. Rosie and Andrea needed no instruction. They both rushed inside the hiding place and waited impatiently for Al to swing the armoire back into place. Andrea was sure she could hear stealthy noises in the hotel hallway just outside the suite.

Big Al struggled with the door of the armoire. For some unexplained reason it refused to budge. "Help me, kid!" he called. Trying to close the armoire from inside was more difficult than having someone on the other side push it closed. It required brute strength just to budge it. Big Al and Andrea struggled with it and Andrea felt a panic begin to churn in her stomach. What if they couldn't get it closed and were discovered? Andrea struggled a bit harder and the door suddenly swung shut, not a moment too soon.

As the armoire snapped into place, cleverly concealing the people behind it, the hotel suite door burst
open. "This is a raid!" Andrea heard for the second time
that night, and then the sound of rushing feet followed.

Angry words and swearing could be heard as the
police searched the suite in vain. They would find
nothing, Andrea realized, and she was glad. She
refused to think about the legal issues of Prohibition
and gangsters. She would adopt a new motto, she
decided: live and let live. If she lived by that, she
would never have to think about what was right and
wrong; or legal and illegal things; or good and bad
people. When she thought about things like that, life
really got complicated. This way she could just feel
happy that she had kept Big Al and Rosie from getting into trouble. So she set her mind firmly on that
and refused to let it budge.

After a few minutes Big Al placed a warm hand on
her shoulder and motioned her to follow him. Silent
as tiny night creatures, Rosie, Big Al, and Andrea
crept into the tunnel and away from the police and
the Hazleton Hotel. They walked on, a curious hud-
dle of people, the man's hands placed protectively
around Rosie's shoulders. They passed four lamps
before Big Al felt confident enough to speak. "I really
owe ya big time, kid," he said. "You saved my skin!"

"And mine, twice," Rosie added. "What's yer
name?" She smiled kindly at Andrea.

They had come to rest under the fourth lantern and it shone above them, giving them the opportunity to study one another's features. "Andy," Andrea replied instantly. She was now used to being called by that name. Big Al tipped his head slightly, and Andrea shivered. She could almost feel his powerful fist clenching in anger. "And-Andrea," she quickly amended. "Andrea," she repeated more firmly and fearfully returned his gaze.

"Thank you, Andrea," he smiled. Even in the gloomy tunnel, Andrea could see that the smile did not reach his eyes. They remained hard and cold, sending a queer little shiver of misgiving tickling feather-soft down her spine.

"A girl?!" Rosie gasped, and then she laughed. "Good for you, sweetheart. It's about time us women did something for ourselves! I told ya you were a cute boy. I knew there was something soft about ya!"

"The police are going to be looking all over town for you," Andrea reminded Big Al. "What are you going to do? Are we safe here?"

"Yeah, we're safe down here unless someone snitched!" He turned brittle cold eyes back to Andrea. "How did you find out anyway?" he demanded.

"Oh, I-I –" Andrea stuttered absurdly. She hadn't even thought that he might ask her that question and she had no ready reply.

"Oh Al, leave the kid alone," Rosie interjected, taking Scarface by the arm.

Al roughly shook Rosie's hand off his sleeve and shoved her aside. He took a menacing step toward Andrea, his large hands ready to grab her throat. "Well?" he demanded.

Andrea was saved from answering. A distinct scuffing sound could be heard echoing through the tunnel. "Quick, against the wall," Al ordered, "and be quiet, if ya know what's good for ya."

Andrea took the opportunity to slide along the tunnel wall as far away from Big Al and Rosie as she could get. She knew that Al had had to let the matter drop, but he would ask her again, and she had better have a ready answer. She decided that she wouldn't tell him about the snitch, Joe, even though she thought he was a weasel. Something told her that Big Al would stop at nothing to get revenge, and Andrea didn't want that on her conscience.

The noises faded away. It sounded to Andrea as if someone had been running through another part of the tunnel system and the sounds had echoed into distant tunnels. Big Al must have thought the same thing too, for he didn't look too concerned. After a few minutes Andrea heard Big Al speak. "Looks like the heat's on again," he laughed. "It's nuthin' I ain't seen before. Guess I'll high-tail it outta town for a month or two. Take the train back down to Chicago – see if the cops have missed me down there." He seemed to have forgotten all about being angry at Andrea and wanting information.

Rosie sighed an audible sigh and Big Al turned to her. "Aw, come on, Rosie. You know you're my best girl." He put his arms around her and pulled her close.

That was when Andrea decided that three was a crowd. She deliberately turned her back on the two of them and walked purposely toward the next lantern. Everything about Big Al was beginning to disgust her, and she found that she didn't even want to be in the same tunnel with him. He had pushed Rosie away when she had tried to help Andrea. What would he have done to Andrea if the scurrying noises in the tunnel hadn't distracted him? Andrea shuddered, thinking about it.

Unfortunately, Andrea knew that she just couldn't walk away from Big Al. He would probably come after her and exact some sort of revenge on her. So she slowed her footsteps and waited for Big Al and Rosie at the next lantern. She bided her time by scuffing first one toe and then the other in the dirt floor of the tunnel, awaiting her next orders. She smoothed her tousled, grit-filled hair, wondering if she would ever be able to wash the dirt out. She waited for a few minutes and, when they didn't catch up with her, she continued to the next lantern. Before long Andrea found herself at the intersection of the Windy tunnel and the one that crossed under Main Street. Should she go on alone? Would Big Al want her to work again tonight? Andrea paused, wondering what to do. She hesitated, trying to decide whether to turn into the next tunnel or wait. It was then that she heard the same scuffing sounds in the tunnel again. Was it the cops?!

Andrea held her breath, listening to the sounds. This time they kept coming closer and closer. Her heart jumped in her throat and she stood frozen to the spot. For once, her exhausted and overworked brain went on strike. She couldn't think! The sounds grew louder and more distinct. Whoever it was would turn the corner any second now.

Suddenly Andrea's mind jumped into action. She plastered herself against the wall of the tunnel, hoping against hope that the intruder would be so intent on finding the end of the tunnel, he would run right past her. Andrea held her breath. She wanted to close her eyes, but they were stuck wide open watching the whole scene unfold before her in vivid reality.

The interloper came around the corner at breakneck speed and was three metres or more past before Andrea realized who it was. "Vance!" she cried, barely recognizing him in the gloom. Her voice echoed wildly in the tunnel.

Vance yelled and jumped straight into the air. He scraped his head on the ceiling and something flew out of his hand. It hit the dirt ceiling before dropping to the floor of the tunnel. If it hadn't been so serious, Andrea would have collapsed from laughter and relief. He looked so comical, arms and legs flailing in every direction. "Don't scare me like that!" he shouted when he could speak. He turned around and grabbed Andrea by the arm. "Where's Ol' Scarface!?" he demanded brusquely. "Is it too late?!"

"Sh-h-h," Andrea reminded him, glancing back into the gloom. She remembered how the tunnels carried sounds and was afraid they would be overheard.

"I heard shoutin' and yellin' at Scotty's just now. Someone said something about Ol' Scarface and the Hazleton. I was just on my way over there to warn Big Al when ya scared me witless!"

"No, it wasn't too late," Scarface replied roughly as he stepped into the small circle of light with Rosie in tow. Andrea got the impression that he had been standing just out of sight eavesdropping on their conversation. "Why are you so concerned about it being too late, boy?" he snarled menacingly. "Who wants ta know? Somebody after my job? Who are you workin' for?" He poked Vance in the chest with a stubby finger.

"I work for you," Vance replied firmly. He stood his ground even though Andrea could tell he was terrified.

"Andr – ah – Andy here saved the day!" Rosie announced trying to diffuse the suddenly tense situation.

Vance clapped Andy on the back, new respect in his eyes. "I guess yer one of us now! I got worried when I couldn't find ya. Then I found this." Vance bent once more to pick up his battered, filthy cap and handed it to Andrea.

"I gotta catch the midnight train," Big Al interrupted, "or I'd teach you a thing or two!" He shook his fist in Vance's direction. "You better watch yourself, boy. Ya never know who could be comin' after ya."

"Al," Rosie admonished timidly. "Vance is a good kid, he was only tryin' ta help us out."

Al snorted, jerking away from Rosie. "Mind yer own business," he growled. "Yer lucky, kid." He stared at both Vance and Andrea, pinning them to the tunnel wall with his glacial gaze, and then seemed to make a decision. "I ain't got time for this right now," he muttered and let the matter drop. "You two have jobs to do. You," Big Al pointed to Vance, "take Rosie here down the tunnel on the other side of Main. Take her to the surface and see her home and come back the same way. Got that?"

Vance nodded, looking somewhat confused. "Sure," he agreed, "but wh–"

"Don't ask questions, boy!" Big Al growled raising his fist.

Vance nodded mutely, turning to Rosie. "Ready to go?"

Rosie's eyes were bright jewels of unshed tears reflecting in the flickering light. "Ready as I'll ever be!" She laughed, and it made a sad hollow sound that echoed through the tunnel. "Goodbye, Al," she said brokenly. Her voice quivered. Andrea could feel her pain. "I enjoyed every minute of it." Rosie touched two fingers to her lips, then pressed them against Al's cheek. Her movement caused the light to bounce off a beautiful necklace and pendant hanging around her neck. It shimmered in the lantern light, catching Al's attention. He gently touched it with one finger. "The necklace is beautiful," Rosie whispered, clasping his hand. "Thank you, Al."

"Anything for my best girl." Al declared, more loudly this time. It rang weak and hollow in Andrea's ear. It sounded as if he were just saying the words that he thought Rosie wanted to hear. "See ya 'round, Rosie," he threw out, carelessly shifting back and forth from one foot to the other. Somehow he didn't look like a forlorn lover about to depart on a long trip, perhaps to never see his girlfriend again. But then, maybe Andrea had watched too many modern Hollywood movies. Scarface leaned over to embrace Rosie once more.

While Big Al and Rosie were busy saying their last goodbyes, Vance took the opportunity to speak to Andrea. "Meet me at the tunnel junction on the other side of Main," he whispered not wanting Ol' Scarface to overhear.

"You mean near that forbidden tunnel?" Andrea whispered back.

Vance nodded. "It'll probably take me longer than you, but wait for me there. It's been a long night, lots of excitement. I'm beat and ready to go home. What about you?"

Andrea nodded forlornly. She'd forgotten that she couldn't just "go home" tonight. She couldn't have a nice hot shower and sleep in her own comfortable bed. She'd have to sleep wherever Vance found room for her in his overcrowded house. At least, Andrea assumed it would be overcrowded and small. Isn't that what most houses were like in the 1920s, unless your family was super rich?

"I don't understand why Ol' Scarface wants me ta use that forbidden tunnel," Vance mused quietly. "It's only used for emergencies and storage and such. Something just isn't adding up. Oh well…." He let the matter drop when he saw Scarface and Rosie turn toward them.

"Okay, boy, get going," Scarface interrupted Vance's thoughts, almost pushing Rosie into his skinny adolescent arms. He pulled his watch out of his pocket and pointedly studied it. "See ya 'round, Rosie," he said dismissing her totally. He slowed his pace to let Rosie and Vance go on ahead in the dark tunnel. Weird, thought Andrea. He's acting very strange right now. She stood in the gloom with Ol' Scarface, watching Rosie and Vance trudge along until the tunnel swallowed them up completely. She saw Rosie turn once and raise her hand in farewell, the necklace winking faintly like a tiny pinprick of light in the gloom. Her cheeks glistened slightly and Andrea knew that they were wet with tears.

Big Al and Andrea stood watching until the other two were out of sight. Then Big Al did an about-face and started heading back to the Hazleton again. "Where are we going?!" The words burst out of Andrea's mouth before she could clamp her teeth shut. "I thought you wanted to get to the train station."

Big Al spun around and glared down at her. "Where I want ta go is my business, Missy. You just mind. Remember, I'm the boss." His words were like steel.

"Sure," Andrea conceded quickly, trying to avoid his sudden flare of anger. "I just thought –"

"That's the trouble with ya," Big Al broke in. "Ya think too much. Leave that ta me, ya got that? Otherwise you and me are gonna have a short partnership. I don't take kindly ta the likes of anyone advisin' me unless I ask! Just because ya saved my skin doesn't give ya the right ta question me, got that?" His thoughts suddenly turned. "Just how did ya find out about that raid anyway?" he asked darkly.

"I-I just overheard it," Andrea replied, avoiding the mention of names. She had had time to think of an answer that wouldn't give Joe away and now she used it. "I heard the cops talking together," she lied. "They didn't see me. I-I was hidden in the shadows on the platform waiting for my next trip."

"Well, ya did save my neck, kid," Ol' Scarface said cheerfully, buying her story. He had totally forgotten that he had been angry with her just two minutes before. "I woulda been a goner if it wasn't for you. You got guts, girlie." He put a fatherly arm about her shoulders and they walked on together in silence.

His arm should have been a comfort, Andrea thought, but it wasn't. It felt heavy and uncomfortable, and somehow full of power and barely restrained anger. It didn't feel at all like her own father's arm, which was so loving and warm. It made Andrea feel homesick and lonely for her large, happy, consistent family. She always knew where she stood with them. They never left her guessing about anything, especially their love for her. Even crazy old Aunt Bea, with her weird clothes and mannerisms.

Big Al and Andrea walked along, getting ever closer to the Hazleton. They stopped almost by unspoken consent, just under one of the last lanterns. Big Al absentmindedly played with something in his pocket. He seemed to be trying to make some kind of decision.

"I really owe ya big time," Al commented quietly. "And I wanted ta reward ya for helping me out." He pulled his hand out of his pocket, his fingers clenched in a fist. With his other hand he reached for her palm, gently opened it flat, and placed something in it. "I gave Rosie a choice and she picked the other one," he said, "so I'm giving ya this one to say thanks." Big Al pulled his hand away and revealed a necklace nesting in the palm of her hand. It sparkled and winked in the lantern light, looking very expensive, even to Andrea's untrained eye.

"B-but – but," Andrea stuttered. "I-I can't accept this." She stared at the beautiful pendant glimmering in the weak light.

"It's yours," Al replied gruffly, stopping all further argument. "Don't argue with me, girlie," he uttered in a dangerously soft tone. "You know what happens to people who cross me." Andrea stood stock still, her eyes round in terror. So this was how it happened. This was how innocent, decent, law-abiding people got caught up in the dark side of life. It started out as a friendly game and somehow became a sticky spider web of threats and lies and innuendo; of gifts that became bribes to buy false loyalty. Suddenly the innocent person was trapped, webs of deceit ensnaring the captive – the guileless insect imprisoned and powerless against the advancing spider.

"Here, let me help you put it on," Big Al spoke quietly. He carefully took the necklace out of her nerveless hand and expertly fastened it around her neck. "Ya sure had me fooled," he chuckled as he worked at getting the necklace hooked. "All dungarees, short hair, and cap. It wasn't till ya screamed that I knew ya was a girl! Ya sure are tough for a girl!"

Andrea felt the pendant weighing heavy on her chest. "Th-thank you," she felt obliged to whisper, her eyes filled with anxiety. She didn't like the idea of accepting any kind of gift from Ol' Scarface. She felt as if she was being bought for a price.

Big Al backed away, studying her in the dim lantern light. "It's also ta mark yer promotion in the business, see."

"Promotion?" Andrea wanted to be pleased at the thought of advancing so quickly with Ol' Scarface and his organization, but something worrisome tugged at her stomach muscles, screaming, to be acknowledged. This promotion just didn't feel right. "Wh-what about Vance?" she asked timidly, afraid of the man's wrath.

Big Al snorted. "You leave Vance ta me! He'll be taken care of – needs ta be brought down a peg or two – just wouldn't mind me."

Suddenly Andrea exploded, fear and concern for Vance invading her body. "What have you done with him?" she demanded. "He's my friend! I can't just take his job away – that'd be so sneaky and underhanded and unfair! Vance would never do that to me – I won't take your promotion –"

A loud thwack bounced off the tunnel walls cutting Andrea's tirade dead on her trembling lips. In his anger and fury Old Scarface had punched the dirt wall. Andrea flinched and cowered into the opposite wall as far away from the raging man as possible. He could have just as easily punched me, Andrea realized with a shudder. She studied the hole in the far wall, her body quaking with fear.

"Ya watch yer mouth, girlie. Unless ya want ta end up like Vance at the end of some dead-end tunnel!" Old Scarface growled dangerously and sprang at Andrea. He grabbed her hair and twisted it tightly against her scalp.

"N-n-no," Andrea moaned. She meant no, she wouldn't take Vance's job.

But Big Al took it to mean that she was agreeing with his way of thinking, that she didn't want to end up anymore hurt than she already was. "I'm glad ya can see some sense, girl." He released her once more and pushed her back into the tunnel wall. "Nobody says no ta me – got that, kid? Not you, not my Ma, not nobody. Yer workin' fer me now, and there ain't no way out of it except…." Big Al glared icily into her terrified eyes as his threat slowly seeped into her paralyzed brain. Would he actually kill her, she wondered in fright, if, she refused to take the job?

"Don't test me, kid." His voice was deadly calm and quiet. It terrified her to think that he could actually read her mind. "I don't play games with nobody. Ya do it my way, always. That's what ya need ta remember ta succeed, to survive in this business. If ya do that, ya won't get inta hot water." He laughed low and sinister from deep within his throat, causing the hairs on Andrea's arms to stand up in alarm.

The evil sound echoed around the enclosed tunnel, penetrating Andrea's very soul as she stood shivering in the eerie gloom. It had finally, permanently, sunk in. She realized now how dangerous this man was, how scared she was, how very much alone she was. If he killed her now, no one would ever find her. She would never make it back home and her parents would always wonder what had become of her. They would never guess in a million years that she had been transported back in time.

Andrea only wanted to go home. She wanted to return to a world that she understood. She wanted more than anything to be surrounded by her cheerful, caring family. She wondered despondently if she would ever get her wish.

"And another thing," Ol' Scarface chose that moment to break into Andrea's thoughts. "If ya want ta succeed, forget this friend business. There ain't no such thing as a good friend. Everybody's out ta get what they can in life. That includes you, me, and your so-called friend, Vance." He took a quick step toward Andrea grabbing her throat with one thick, strong hand. "Ya ain't got no friend but me now, got that, girlie?" Andrea nodded mutely and swallowed thickly. She could feel her throat move against Ol' Scarface's hand. Her eyes watered with unshed tears. "You be a good friend to Big Al, ya hear? Ya just might have ta die fer me someday." With that Al laughed wickedly and released

Andrea's throat. He turned away and casually sauntered up the tunnel as if nothing had happened.

ANDREA'S MIND WAS IN A TOTAL FOG of fear and confusion. She followed Big Al on rubbery legs back to the Hazleton Hotel, panic sitting on her chest making her breathing laboured. Fear pumped through her body, pooling into her numb fingertips. Who was this evil man?! Andrea would not have been surprised to discover that there were actually two Al's, and this one was the evil twin brother. Where had this man come from? she wondered. How had he managed to fool her so well? She felt sick and disgusted with herself. She had fallen for some dangerous criminal's "nice guy" act and was now in grave danger. Not only that, what had happened to Vance? Andrea was so anxious about his safety. What if – Andrea pushed that horrible thought out of her head. She must concentrate on keeping herself safe. As soon as possible, she would go search for Vance. That was all she could do at the moment. She needed to be cool and calm and get away from Ol' Scarface as quickly as possible.

The pendant around her neck bounced against her chest as she walked, serving as a constant reminder that she had sold herself for a lousy piece of jewellery. An expensive one, to be sure, but she loathed it just the same. It wasn't a gift given with gratitude or affection.

It was a bribe. Andrea couldn't wait to take the stupid thing off her neck and throw it as far away as she could. She wanted to grind it into the gravel crunching beneath her feet. But she knew that Big Al might ask to see it sometime, just to make sure that she still had it. So, playing it safe, she carefully tucked the offending necklace beneath the neck of her T-shirt until she could find a safe hiding place for it. She didn't want Vance to notice it. He was sure to know who had given it to her and it wouldn't take him long to figure out that Big Al was planning to have Andrea take over his job.

She trudged along after Big Al, her thoughts whirling. Oh Vance, where are you? Andrea cried silently in the dark tunnel. She could just discern Big Al's broad back and shoulders several metres in front of her. She glared at his retreating body, wishing that she could make him tell her where Vance was and what he had done with him. Vance was more of a friend than Big Al could ever possibly be! Vance knew how to be a true friend. Big Al was actually a dictator, a power wielding creep who tried to buy and bribe friendship and loyalty. And when that didn't work, he threatened. Andrea hoped and prayed that she would never have to see him again after this terrifying trip.

They came at last to the Hazleton Hotel's secret entrance. Big Al was still several metres in front of Andrea. He stood placidly by the concealed door while Andrea slowly caught up. "Done sulkin' now, are ya?"

Andrea quickly nodded, not wanting to set him off again. "Yes, sir," she replied politely through stiff lips. She couldn't look him in the eye, though, she was afraid that he would see just how much she despised him.

"Yer job's done here for the night," he dismissed her, leisurely tossing a coin in her direction. It bounced off Andrea's nerveless fingers and fell into the dirt at her feet. "Go to The Four Star Café tomorrow evening about seven o'clock for yer night's assignments. Don't forget," he paused for a few seconds, "or run away...."

Ol' Scarface knocked out the code on the hidden door while Andrea debated what to do. She wanted to stomp the coin into the gravel, burying it far beneath her feet. She wanted to show this horrible man just what she would like to do to him. But that would be dangerous. Andrea took a deep calming breath and bent to run her fingers over the surface of dirt and sand beneath her feet searching for the coin.

The door opened while Andrea still knelt. Light spilled into the area, bouncing off the missing coin. Andrea picked it up. Holding it in her hand, she rose slowly, glancing toward the light, watching as Big Al entered the room. "What took ya so long, Al?" Andrea heard a feminine voice coo. "I was gettin' bored without ya. I wasn't sure you'd be back after that scare with the cops. I'm so-o-o glad you made it." The voice actually purred! Andrea had read that expression in one of her girlfriend's ridiculous teen romance novels, but could never understand how a human voice could purr. Now she knew. And on top of everything else, the voice did not belong to Rosie! Al was obviously two-timing his "best girl." Andrea had thought that he must care for Rosie at least a little bit, after giving her the necklace and acting all lovey-dovey; now Andrea knew it was just that – an act.

The door started to swing shut, leaving Andrea in its fading light. "Remember, Andy," Big Al's voice floated clearly into the tunnel. "Tomorrow. Don't try ta skip out on me now. Moose Jaw ain't such a big town, ya know. I'd find ya sooner or later…and then…." The door swung shut on his haunting laughter.

Andrea fell heavily and abruptly to the tunnel floor, her trembling legs finally giving out on her. She sat crouched against the wall near the secret entrance, knowing that she wasn't really safe, but unable to trust her legs to move. She felt like an animal, hunted and trapped, caught in a corner waiting to die. Finally, after several minutes, Andrea felt her heart slow to a dull thud. Her brain began to function again. What a fool she had been about Big Al. It was so embarrassing, and it worried her to think that she had been so gullible. Had she actually said that she liked the man!? It was all her fault that Vance was in trouble, and she needed to find him.

That was the thought that got her legs working again. She tested them, carefully pulling herself upright and into a standing position. She walked a few paces, making sure that her knees wouldn't buckle again. When she was sure that she had recovered, she started to sprint through the tunnel, winding her way back to where she had last seen Vance. Andrea flew through Windy tunnel, feeling a strong current of air blowing even as she ran. She ducked into the Main Street tunnel and continued, hunched over and awkward.

As the intersection of the two tunnels drew near, Andrea slowed to a walk. Blood pounded through her veins, reverberating in her head. She could feel her temples pulse with every heartbeat. Andrea stood for a moment where the tunnels crossed, wondering which way to go. To the left was the tunnel to Scotty's Shoe Store and The Four Star Café. To the right lay the forbidden tunnel where Ol' Scarface had instructed Vance to take Rosie.

It had been a strange conversation, Andrea realized, thinking back. Vance had questioned Big Al's judgment, something he hadn't done before, at least not in Andrea's presence. Big Al had been very insistent. He demanded that Vance use the forbidden tunnel, even though it hadn't been an emergency.

Andrea thought about all of this as she stood in the dreary tunnel wondering what to do. Should she wait for Vance here where it was somewhat safe, or should she venture into the forbidden tunnel and risk getting caught?

With her thoughts on Vance, Andrea almost didn't hear it. It sounded like a moan, a low mournful sound that sent shivers down her spine. This place is haunted, Andrea thought. What else but a ghost could create such a ghoulish tone? It was coming from inside the forbidden tunnel, riding on the air currents that blew softly into the intersection.

Andrea stood listening to the sound, trying to decipher it. Was it human or not? It sounded freakish and unreal, like something out of a horror movie. Andrea never watched horror movies, they scared her too much.

It was a human voice, Andrea tried to convince herself. And if it was human, then it was quite possibly Vance. If Vance was hurt, it was Andrea's fault. He had only been trying to help her when he had angered Ol' Scarface at The Four Star Café. By the sounds coming from the tunnel, the person was in really bad shape. Andrea needed to do something. She took one step and then another into the forbidden tunnel. She felt as if she was being drawn in by a force larger than herself. She couldn't stop her feet. They just keep trudging on closer and closer to the sound, as if they followed a different master. I'm doing this for Vance, Andrea reminded herself over and over again, trying to keep other terrifying thoughts at bay. Even if it wasn't Vance, someone needed help, and Andrea was the only one around. It was all up to her.

12:15 AM Saturday Morning

JOURNEY INTO
THE FORBIDDEN TUNNEL

The lanterns were spaced further apart in the forbidden tunnel, probably to discourage anyone from wandering in. Sometimes it was so dark that Andrea couldn't see the hand she put right in front of her face. She thought fleetingly of grabbing a lantern and taking it in with her, but she was afraid that someone would come along behind her and realize that it was gone. That would give definite proof that someone was lurking in the tunnel. Andrea knew that she had to be very careful not to be detected, so she continued through the oppressive blackness. Fear caused her scalp to prickle. Her hair felt as if it was actually standing on end!

The moaning stopped and Andrea found herself in a kind of no man's land. She was between lanterns in the pitch black. All sight and sound had vanished. She could hear the rough panting of her own breath and feel her heart thudding against her chest. It felt as if it was about to leap out and run back down the tunnel all by itself! Andrea couldn't blame it. She felt that way too. What am I doing here? she cried silently. This is crazy! I am not this brave.

Andrea whirled around to flee back to safer points, the very blackness looming over her like an evil shadow. Then she heard a faint cry. It was more like whimper. "Vance?"

In this sightless world, Andrea stretched both hands out to her sides to guide her along. She inched her way along in the narrow tunnel, hands touching the tunnel walls. Blinded by the inky blackness, Andrea walked straight into a dirt wall. Several clumps of earth rained down upon her already filthy clothes. Panic niggled at the edges of her brain. Had she somehow become disoriented and lost in this lightless void?

Willing the panic away, Andrea stretched her arms out and began to feel for an edge. She heard the moaning again and moved toward the sound. Her right hand felt a rough edge and Andrea poked her head cautiously around it. No wonder she couldn't see anything! This tunnel had taken a sharp and unmarked turn, causing Andrea to bump into the wall. Having made the turn, Andrea could now just barely see a weak flickering light way down the tunnel. Even with the dim light, Andrea realized after the first step that she would never find anyone without having a source of light. "Oh I wish I had a flashlight!" she murmured to herself. She would have to get a lantern; there was no other way. She glanced ahead down the tunnel toward the next lantern. It flickered faintly, too dim to give more than the promise of light. She hurried as fast as she could toward it and pulled it off the hook.

Holding it high, Andrea saw that the walls were rough and rocky. They seemed to be more hacked at than the walls in the other tunnels. As she looked around, she noticed that the wall on one side suddenly fell away, revealing a large area carved out underground. The lone lantern cast large eerie shadows into the void. There were many dark spots which Andrea suddenly realized were stacks of wooden boxes and barrels. They're probably full of booze, Andrea thought. There were empties strewn about too in a tangled mess of broken boxes. Barrels were on their sides or stacked two high in places.

The large dug-out area was like an underground cavern. It was supported by many poles that stretched floor to ceiling in an area that seemed to be about the size of two school classrooms laid side by side. It must be connected to some business, Andrea thought, as she strained her eyes in the darkness. She thought she could see a place where a door might be, but the opposite wall was too far away for her to see clearly.

The wounded sound came again, and Andrea jumped. For a moment she had forgotten her rescue mission. Was it Vance who was making such a freakish sound, she wondered. "Vance?" she asked, as she carefully skirted some boxes stacked taller than her head. She peered behind them. "Vance?"

The sound was closer. Andrea scrambled over a few broken and discarded objects and called loudly, "Vance?" She held her lantern high, frantically searching the mess of boxes and barrels.

This time the moan sounded to her immediate right. It was a human sound, Andrea was positive. She was also certain that it was Vance, her gut instinct told her so. Tears gathered in her eyes, and Andrea couldn't see. She reached down, feeling around on the ground. Her hand touched something soft and warm. Andrea squeezed. "Vance!"

"Awwww."

"Sorry," Andrea wailed. "Oh Vance, please talk to me." She set the lantern down and moved her hands as gently but rapidly as possible over his limp body.

"An-And –" His voice was thick with pain.

"Oh Vance," Andrea sobbed. She totally forgot that she was supposed to be a boy. She flung herself down upon his prone body weeping uncontrollably. "Look what I caused. It's all my fault! Oh Vance, are you hurt bad?"

Vance moaned again, but it was an incoherent sound. "I don't know much about first aid, Vance." Andrea lamented. "Please wake up and help me!"

Vance grunted and tried to push her away, mumbling something between bruised lips. Andrea could only understand one word, "boys," but it was enough to make her release Vance and sit up straight. She was supposed to be a boy! Whatever would Vance think of her, hugging him that way!

"Sorry," she mumbled, suddenly embarrassed by her actions. "I was just so happy to see you."

Vance groaned and mumbled again. Andrea thought he might have said, "thanks," but she knew that if he had, he meant it sarcastically. Andrea ran her hands up and down Vance's arms and chest, squeezing. She had suddenly remembered the first aid course she had taken in Guides. "Where does it hurt?" Wasn't that one of the first questions to be asked?

More mumbling. Had he said, "Everywhere"? Andrea reached over to squeeze the arm stretched away from his body in an awkward position, and got quite a reaction. The howl of pain caused her ears to ring as Vance lurched roughly out of her grasp.

"We've got to get you out of here." Andrea suddenly took charge. "Can you sit up?" She gently helped him into a sitting position, leaning his back against a stack of boxes. "Broken arm," she quietly assessed. She looked at it hanging strangely from his shoulder. "We have to do something with that arm before we move you too far. What we need is…." Andrea's voice trailed off as she looked around. She was thankful for the mock emergency situations that she had had to deal with at Guides. They were helping her remain calm and stay in control. She should at least be able to make Vance a little more comfortable and then help get him out of this place.

Andrea picked up the lantern and held it near Vance's face to do a more thorough search for injuries, as her memory kicked into action. This was one of the first things the first aid book had recommended. Andrea gasped as Vance peered at her groggily through one eye. The other was completely swollen shut. Dried blood crusted his upper lip. Andrea felt her eyes fill with tears again. "Still think your friend Scarface is a great man?!" Vance muttered through stiff lips.

"B-b-but," Andrea stammered, "he was with me." She wanted to share all of the conflicting thoughts whirling in her mind, confessing to Vance all that had happened in the tunnel with Ol' Scarface, but she was trying to focus on the problems at hand. She could only deal with one issue at a time right now.

"You still don't get it, do ya?" Vance continued. He looked ready to strangle her, if he had had the strength and the use of both arms. "He didn't do this to me. No. He just gets his henchmen, his goons, ta do it for him – the lily-livered –" Vance stopped suddenly, exhausted. "Never mind," he muttered, leaning back against the boxes, closing his eyes. "I used ta be like you – thought the man walked on water or something. It's taken this to make me realize…I wonder what it'll take until you come ta your senses?"

Andrea sighed and dashed away the tears from her cheeks. She wanted to tell Vance the truth, that she had seen the light. That Big Al was a jerk, worse than a jerk. But she had more important things to do right now, like getting Vance to safety in case the goons came back looking for him.

"We need to do something with your arm," Andrea told Vance. She lifted the lantern and went in search of something to hold it in place. She had already checked her own pockets, finding only the barrettes that she had hastily pulled from her head hours before. She needed a piece of cloth; a scarf or…there! Sticking out from under some boxes Andrea saw a piece of rope. It wasn't ideal. It was a bit too narrow and would bite into Vance's back and shoulder, but it was better than nothing. Andrea grabbed the rope and returned to Vance's side.

How could she be so calm, she wondered, coming once again upon Vance's bruised and battered face. She should be a bundle of nerves and panic. Here she was, suddenly in control of a lousy situation and doing a good job of it too. She could have still been in tears, helpless and wondering what to do. Andrea smiled, suddenly proud of herself. It felt good. Perhaps she was maturing, as her father had said. It seemed like a lifetime since she had seen her family, but Andrea let that thought go. She had to get Vance to safety. She had a job to complete. She needed to bandage Vance's arm to his body for support and then, as quickly as possible, get medical attention. That meant getting him out of the tunnel unnoticed, and that might prove a difficult feat.

Andrea reached for Vance's bad arm and then stopped, suddenly remembering that the patient should do this part if possible. "Vance," she instructed, "move that arm into a comfortable position. Try to put it against your chest." Vance grunted but did as he was told, slowly and painfully moving his arm until it rested, bent at the elbow, against his chest. "I'm going to tie your arm to your chest with this rope." Andrea slid the rope around his back and under his arm, tying it gently but firmly at the shoulder. "How's that?"

Vance never got a chance to answer for strange sounds could suddenly be heard, faint and low, way down the tunnel. "Oh no," Andrea whispered, her fingers frozen on the rope at Vance's neck. "It sounds like voices! We'd better hide quick!" They'd be caught for sure now, Andrea thought.

Vance mumbled something Andrea couldn't understand. "What?" Andrea listened again. "The lantern?"

She looked down at it, sitting in the dirt nearby. "Oh, the lantern, of course." Andrea bent to blow it out. Vance grabbed her shirt and shook his head slowly, in too much pain to move it any faster. "You don't want me to blow it out – but, then what – " Vance was gesturing wildly, as wildly as one can with an arm tied back and a throbbing head. "You want me to put it back?!" Andrea stared at him in disbelief, losing several precious seconds. "But V-Vance, that's stupid. I might run into the guy. Just let me blow it out –"

Vance shook his head firmly. Even Andrea could feel the pain, or at least imagine what it must feel like. Vance uttered something again. It sounded like – "They'd search for the lantern and find us for sure." Vance nodded and Andrea knew he was right! "Tunnel turns, remember," Vance just managed to mumble.

"That's right!" Andrea remembered. She would have time to replace the lantern, but she had to hurry.

Vance suddenly took charge. He cranked the wick down to its lowest point and shoved the lantern into Andrea's frozen fingers. He gave her an awkward one-handed push that got her moving. He was mumbling something and gesturing again, cupping his good hand with his bad one, as if trying to tell her something. But what?

Andrea half crawled, half ran, until she came to the last pile of boxes. They kept her hidden from view. She was safe here, but she had to get the lantern back on its hook. That meant dodging across the tunnel in full view of anyone who happened to be near enough to see.

Vance was still with it, even though he was hurt. He had turned down the wick so that it emitted only enough light for Andrea to see, but not enough, hopefully, for the foot shufflers to realize that the lantern was moving. Andrea listened near the boxes as the sound of voices grew steadily louder. It was hard to tell how far away they were. She peered around the boxes and saw no one coming around the corner of the tunnel. Do it now, she commanded her stiff limbs.

Moving slowly, so that the light wouldn't appear to be shifting, Andrea stood and crossed the area to the tunnel wall. She lifted the lantern, placed it on the hook and then carefully adjusted the flame brighter. Then she sank down beside the pole and peered into the darkness of the tunnel. Was it safe for her to cross again and hide with Vance?

A large shadowy figure suddenly emerged from around the corner. Too late! Andrea was stuck crouched beside the pole. She'd be spotted for sure. Andrea pushed back against the dirt wall, trying to make herself as small as possible. Maybe he wouldn't see her – there was a chance, a minuscule chance. She put her hand down for a moment to steady herself and felt a draft. Where was it coming from? She felt further and discovered a small opening in the tunnel wall. It felt like a rounded out hollow space just big enough for her to hide in. That must have been what Vance was trying to tell her! Andrea rolled to the ground and slid into the tiny space just as the shadow broke apart, becoming two.

"I wonder why Ol' Scarface wanted us to use this tunnel tanight? It's usually off limits."

"Haven't you figured it out yet?"

"What?"

Two men had stopped to talk just under the lantern, mere centimetres from Andrea's hiding spot. She saw their shoes, shiny patent leather, gleaming in the weak light.

"Somethin' big's going on tanight. Rumours are flyin' everywhere. There's talk that some new guy's tryin' to muscle in on Scarface's territory here. There's gonna be a big meetin' tanight in the old warehouse. We've been sent to stake out the building, make sure it's secure. That means no cops and no gangsters hidin' out waitin' ta ambush us."

"You mean, 'No gangsters but us!'" Both men laughed uproariously.

"Sh-h-h," the first one muttered, quieting down. "We sure don't want ta be caught down here, or anywhere near here. That's why we're using this tunnel. Ol' Scarface thinks that the cops are on ta us. They seem to be everywhere tanight, and we don't need anybody gettin' suspicious of us."

"Well, we'd better get movin' then. Ol' Scarface's been real short tempered and mean lately. I don't want ta get into his bad books. He can be downright nasty."

They shuffled through the maze of boxes and barrels, heading toward the far wall where Andrea had thought a door might be. Obviously she was right, for a bright light blazed for a few seconds as the door creaked open. Andrea was left in the familiar darkness when the door shut.

She stayed hidden, afraid that they might return, until she heard scuffling sounds coming from where Vance had been hiding. She scrambled out of the hole and hurried to his side. "Come on, Vance, let's get you out of here. There's no telling how soon those men might come back and I don't want to be here if or when they do. It looks like you were right about something big happening tonight. I just hope we can get out of here before anyone else shows up!"

Andrea put her arm around Vance's back and helped him into a standing position. He leaned heavily on her, moaning softly in her ear with every step. "Oh Vance, what have I done?" she whispered to herself. She must have spoken aloud though, for Vance had obviously heard. He gave her arm a faint squeeze with his good hand. It seemed to say, "It's okay."

They walked slowly, Vance leaning for support on Andrea. They continued north up the forbidden tunnel, passing another four weak lanterns. Andrea found the journey endless and terrifying. She was sure that they would be discovered, and then what? She didn't know and refused to let her imagination speculate.

The tunnel appeared to run into a dead end ahead. Andrea tried to question Vance about it, but he didn't even try to reply. All of his energy seemed to be consumed by walking. She was beginning to think that the blows to his head had left him addled and confused. If the tunnel was indeed a dead end, where did that leave them? How would they get out?

They kept walking toward the tunnel wall straight ahead. "B-but Vance, there's nothing there –" Andrea was saying as they reached the wall. Andrea could see nothing, but Vance pushed carefully on one place and a secret door swung open. It was hidden so well that Andrea would never have guessed it was there. They both hurried through and Andrea quickly shut the door tightly, sighing in relief.

Vance was in control again, sort of. He would get them to safety. They entered a winding tunnel that turned this way and that and then very shortly found themselves at another door. Andrea pushed against it and fell out onto concrete steps. Vance tried to push the door closed behind them but couldn't do it. Andrea realized just how weak he was becoming. She shut the door and climbed the steps after Vance. He mumbled something, pointing up with his good hand. Andrea looked up. A door! It lay across the steps at a very funny angle. What was this? "You want me to open that!?" It looked gigantic and heavy.

Vance sighed audibly through sore lips. Andrea pushed on the door. It was at a terrible angle and was very heavy. She grunted and it budged. Andrea climbed another step heaving with all her strength. A crack appeared. Hot humid night air rushed in to greet them. It felt like a sticky wet towel pushing against Andrea's face. Still, it was fresh air and it felt better than the horrid stale tunnel air. But where were they? Of course, Andrea smiled as she heaved the door up. She climbed the last step and looked around at the real world. She realized that she and Vance had just come through an outside entrance to the cellar of a house, just like the one at Grandpa Talbot's.

When the door was open wide enough, Vance scrambled through, carefully protecting his arm. Andrea followed, letting the huge awkward door down as softly as possible. After all, they didn't want to draw attention to their arrival. They were at the back of a large house. The windows were all dark except for a faint light shining from a window on the top floor. Andrea noticed that all of the windows were open on this side of the house, as if someone were trying to catch the breeze. "Where are we?" Andrea wanted to know. "At your house?"

Vance shook his head and motioned for Andrea to follow him. They slipped around the side of the house, as quietly as two shadows in the night sky. James Bond would be proud of me, Andrea thought. They reached the front of the house and crept like two mice up the wide steps. Vance opened the screen door slowly and Andrea moved in to turn the handle of the inner door. It released easily and swung open.

"Why are we here?" Andrea whispered as they scaled the stairs. "Who lives here?"

Andrea didn't have to wait long to find out. They crept past the first and second floors and kept climbing, coming to the landing where a door blocked the way. Vance tapped softly and the door flew open, blinding the two in the sudden brightness of light. "Oh Vance!" Hands reached out to grab them, bringing them into the kitchen of the suite.

Rosie! Andrea gasped and stared. Gone was the heavy make-up and neat hair style. Gone too was the gaudy feather boa and tight dress. Instead Andrea saw a pretty, fresh-faced girl. Why, she looked barely eighteen! Rosie wrapped a large dressing gown more tightly around her waist and stood staring at Vance in dismay.

"Ice!" Andrea demanded angrily. "We need ice for his face!"

"Ice?!" Rosie snorted. "Where do ya think we'd find ice in July!? This ain't the Ritz, ya know. And I doubt they'd even have it today, it's so hot!"

"You must have ice in the refrigerator!" Andrea

retorted, angry at being laughed at when she was trying to help. She pushed her way roughly around Rosie and stood in the middle of the small tidy kitchen looking for the fridge.

"Refrigerator?!" Rosie eyed Andrea skeptically. "Where are you from?" she asked slowly, her eyes piercing a hole into Andrea's trembling heart.

"We need ice," Andrea repeated mechanically, spying a small box that could have been a refrigerator in the corner of the room. It hit her suddenly. That was an ice box. There were no refrigerators; not like the kind she was used to with instant ice, cubed or crushed, at the push of a button. Rosie was right, of course. In July in the 1920s, there would be no ice to speak of. In her concern for Vance, Andrea had made a terrible mistake.

She turned back slowly, wondering how to explain her blunder. Rosie and Vance both stared at her as if she were from Mars. Vance mumbled something that Andrea could not decipher.

"Yeah," Rosie agreed with him. It was obvious that she could understand him better than Andrea could. "You sure are strange! Just where are you from?"

If only they knew, Andrea thought. What would they think of instant ice, instant coffee, or cold drinks in the blink of an eye?

"What about cool cloths?" Andrea ignored their questioning glances. She had no answer that they would want to hear. They wouldn't believe her if she told them the truth. She barely believed it herself, and she was the one living it!

Rosie jumped into action then, pushing Andrea aside and finding cloths to bathe Vance's eye. She hustled him into a high-backed wooden chair near the table and fussed over him like a mother hen over her chick. "You went back into that tunnel, didn't ya?" she gently admonished as she pressed a cool wet cloth against his black eye. "I told you not to." She shook her head.

"Why didn't ya listen to me?" Rosie continued. "I told you Al was up to somethin'. I know him better than you do." Andrea snorted from her corner by the door where she had been pushed during the commotion. She wondered if Rosie could guess where Big Al was now, and with whom. Maybe Rosie didn't know him as well as she thought she did.

Vance's groan of pain brought Andrea out of her daydreaming. Rosie was fiddling with the rope around his shoulder, trying to undo the knot she had hurriedly tied. "He needs medical care," she informed Rosie sternly. "I don't think we need to call an ambulance, but we should get him in for X-rays as soon as possible. Why did we come here anyway, Vance? You need medical attention."

Rosie left Vance and walked slowly over to Andrea, her hands on her hips. She studied Andrea as if she were a bizarre creature in the zoo. At least that's what Andrea felt like. Rosie's sharp gaze pinned Andrea to the corner, holding her captive. "Where did Al drag you in from?" Rosie folded her arms under her ample breasts and glared at Andrea. "You ain't from around here, that's for sure." She paused for a moment, her eyes narrowing.

"We might get ol' Doc Anderson ta have a look at Vance to set his arm. But X-rays? Medical attention?" Rosie mimicked Andrea's voice perfectly, continuing to stare at her as if she were looking at a ghost. "You scare me," Rosie admitted.

Vance was mumbling frantically, trying desperately to search his pants pockets. Andrea still couldn't understand a word, though Rosie seemed to. "Money," Rosie interpreted. "You lost it in the tunnel?" Vance nodded. "It fell out of your pocket?"

Rosie stood up and came back in Andrea's direction. "Looks like this is a job for you." Rosie said reluctantly. It was obvious that she didn't trust Andrea, but at the moment she had no other choice.

"What?" Andrea wanted to know.

"Go back into the tunnel and get Vance's money. It must have fallen out of his pocket when they beat him up. It should still be down there, but you'll need to hurry. You don't want somebody else to find it."

"It's dangerous down there!" Andrea practically shouted, suddenly realizing how exhausted and terrified she was. "Those men are nearby and we heard them talking about a big meeting! It's too risky! I won't do it." She didn't want to return to that forbidden tunnel ever again. "It's just money – just a few coins. I don't even think it'd add up to much –"

Suddenly the room was deathly still. Two pair of eyes swung Andrea's way, incredulous looks on ashen faces. "Money is very important if ya ain't got any," Rosie bit out between clenched teeth. "Do you think Vance enjoys gettin' beat up like this? Do ya think he does it for fun? No, he does it because his family needs the money for food and clothes and rent. You must be some rich snob Al brought with him from Chicago. X-rays! Refrigerators!" Rosie snorted. "You get that money, mind now! And don't you come back till you got it all!"

She glared in Andrea's direction, but talked to Vance. "How many coins, Vance? Twenty, ya figure?" She turned back to Andrea. "Twenty coins, got that? Now get going and don't come back till you've got them all!"

Andrea stood frozen to the spot, her mind a blank until Rosie took a threatening step toward her. She jumped into action then, darting out the door, and down the steps into the night air. She didn't slow down until she was around the house near the cellar doors. "I need a flashlight," Andrea muttered again as she leaned against the house trying to decide what to do. The idea of going back into the forbidden tunnel just to pick up a few coins really confounded her. Did the money really mean that much to Vance and his family?

Did it really amount to that much cash? It must, Andrea decided, or people wouldn't be risking their lives or hers to get it!

"I really could use a flashlight," Andrea lamented for the third time. It was good that she hadn't mentioned that thought aloud in the cozy apartment. Rosie had looked very angry and scared and Andrea could understand why. It must have seemed very strange indeed to have a person talking so casually about items that were not commonplace in everyday life in the 1920s. How could she have been so stupid as to demand ice in such a blatant way? Talk about blowing her cover. No wonder Rosie didn't trust her. Andrea knew that she wouldn't have trusted herself in the same circumstances either.

The curtains fluttered in the third floor window, revealing Rosie's determined face. She saw Andrea leaning against the house below and wordlessly waved her toward the tunnel entrance. Even in the dark, Andrea could read the confused yet protective look on her face. She sure seemed to care a lot about Vance. Maybe they were related or something. Andrea wondered briefly if Rosie would ask a lot of questions when she got back and demand logical answers. "I could just run away from this place," Andrea grumbled angrily. She didn't need this hassle, or the danger. She was tired, exhausted in fact, and very frightened. She could just leave. These people were not her responsibility.

The idea sounded good, but Andrea knew that she could never do it. She did owe Vance a lot. It was because of her that he had been beaten. All right, she silently decided, I'll go back and get the stupid coins if it's the last thing I do. She pushed away from the wall and walked toward the cellar entrance. This was what being a true friend was about, she thought, suddenly feeling good about herself. Good friends helped one another, even if they didn't want to; even if it was hard work; even if it was dangerous. And she would help Vance now because it needed to be done, even if it meant going back into the tunnels one last time. She just hoped that the bad guys were long gone. The last thing she needed was to run into them again.

Andrea thought about Rosie too. She was proving to be a good friend to Vance. Boy, was she ever a changed person! She sure took charge of a situation and she was tough and stubborn. Andrea wouldn't want to have to tangle with her! Actually, she liked this Rosie much better than the simpering little doll face she had first met in the tunnels. This Rosie looked like she knew her own mind and would go after what she wanted. Andrea knew that she had better not cross her – she just might need to have Rosie on her side.

Andrea waved a hand of acquiescence in Rosie's direction and pulled the heavy door open. She slipped quietly into the dark space. Supporting the door on her back and shoulders, she walked carefully down the steps, slowly letting the heavy door close softly so that it wouldn't bang and attract unwanted attention. Andrea waited a few moments for her eyes to adjust to the blackness. She listened carefully at the door to the tunnel entrance. Hearing nothing, she slipped like a mole through the door and back into the forbidden tunnel, feeling as if she were Peter Pan, walking the plank over a pit of hungry predators. It was an ominous warning that Andrea wanted to listen to, but she had to get Vance's coins. She had made a promise and she meant to keep it.

Andrea didn't know whether to hurry along the tunnel to find the coins and get out fast and risk being heard, or take her time, moving slowly and cautiously so that she wouldn't be heard. She chose a little of both, travelling fairly quickly past the first couple of lanterns. She walked as quietly as possible, trying not to shuffle her feet or kick up loose gravel as she moved. Surely she would hear anyone coming before they discovered her! At least that's what she hoped.

Andrea kept her mind on the job. To find twenty coins in the dust and gravel of the large dug-out area would be no easy task. She didn't even know exactly where the fight had taken place. The coins could be anywhere in that mess of boxes and barrels and empty bottles. How would she ever find them?

It seemed no time at all before Andrea found herself standing near the lantern that she had so hastily replaced a short time ago. She stood just outside the pale circle of light and listened for several moments before making her move. Sure that no one was waiting or watching, Andrea carefully turned down the wick to diminish the amount of light shining, and lifted the lantern from its hook.

Andrea searched the tunnel area first and found nothing. She had hoped that a nice neat pile of coins would be sitting there just waiting for her. Of course, luck would not make it so, and she turned her attention to the many stacks of boxes and barrels lying about the storeroom. She started closest to the tunnel and searched around every box, every piece of broken casing, and every bottle and barrel. Nothing. She searched around the bottom of the poles used to support the dirt ceiling. Nothing!

Andrea sighed and switched the lantern to her other hand, wiping her sweating palm on her dirty overalls. She felt herself getting more nervous by the second. The longer she spent here, the more at risk she was of being discovered. And if she didn't find the coins, Rosie would be none too pleased either. She was really caught between a rock and a hard place. Andrea grinned at the expression she had heard her Grandfather use before. Now she knew what he meant!

Andrea returned her attention to the ground. She was concentrating so much on the small circle of light thrown out by the lantern, that she didn't realize how close she was coming to the wall at the end of the large cavern. Barrels were mostly piled back here. They had been scattered haphazardly around, as if there had been a fight. This was the area! Andrea lifted the lantern higher and squinted her eyes. There, near a barrel lying on its side, was that something?

Andrea skirted the tumbled remains of boxes and bottles to kneel in the dirt near the barrels. Half buried in the gravel and dirt on the cavern floor were several coins. She placed the lantern on the ground and quickly picked up the money, counting softly out loud as she went. "One, two, three, four." Andrea shoved these into her pocket and ran her hands carefully over the dusty area. "Five, six, seven." She shoved these into her pocket as well and crawled around the area on hands and knees in search of more. "Ouch." Her knee must have landed on a piece of sharp wood. No, it was more coins! "Eight, nine, ten, eleven."

Andrea stayed on her hands and knees, crawling around in the small area. She seemed to have more success that way. She carefully lifted a broken box. Someone had obviously thrown it in a fit of anger. "Twelve, thirteen, fourteen." These she stuffed in her pocket with the others. Andrea was frantic now, she needed to find six more coins! She raced around on her knees, feeling with her hands on the ground. The coins had to be here, but where?

Of course! Maybe some had fallen out of Vance's

pocket where he lay when she had found him. Where was that? It all looked so much the same with the stacks of boxes and barrels all around. Andrea stood for a moment stretching her stiff body and then lifted the lantern over her head to get a better look at the place. A wall! Andrea suddenly saw it in the faint light. She was less than three metres from the wall. And steps. Three rough wooden steps that led into the wall. There must be a door concealed right there, a door which led into an old warehouse, she thought.

Andrea stood stock still, holding the lantern high. She stared at the steps. There, just beneath the bottom stair was something shiny, glittering faintly in her direction. A coin! Andrea had to get it. Where there was one, there might be others.

She put the lantern down and knelt in the dirt again. Leaving the lantern, she got down flat on her stomach and wiggled the few metres, stretching her hand out to reach the coin. "Fifteen," she whispered. "Sixteen, seventeen, eighteen...."

But, where were the other two coins?! Andrea wildly brushed the dust and dirt away but found nothing. Two more coins. She couldn't leave until she had them all. Andrea wiggled closer to the step, sticking her hand right under it. She felt around, first on one side of the large space and then on the other. Nothing! She sighed. What now? She pulled her hand slowly out. It brushed against something. A coin? Andrea dragged the something out in a handful of dirt and gravel. Still lying on her stomach, she opened her hand and blew the dust away. There, glittering in her filthy palm lay not one, not two, but three coins. "Nineteen, twenty and twenty-one!" Andrea wanted to shout and jump up and down. Instead, she wiggled quickly back to the lantern and stood, stuffing the coins, gravel and all, into her pocket.

All of that money, dirt, and gravel created a huge bulge. Andrea cupped her hand around it, over the jeans, material and all. It was about the size of a small snowball, just right for throwing at her little brother. More light-hearted than she had felt in many hours, Andrea picked up the lantern and began to walk between the boxes and barrels toward the opposite tunnel wall. She noticed with faint amusement that the coins rattled and clinked with every step. Just what she needed in a place where every sound could be heard and traced. But she'd found them. All twenty of the coins. And even one more! Wouldn't Rosie and Vance be proud!

Andrea was so involved in congratulating herself on finding not just twenty coins, but twenty-one, that she missed the warning signs. Faint voices and muffled sounds of laughter filtered through the wooden door, growing louder and louder. The metal latch rattled menacingly as the door scraped open, spilling light into the cavernous storage area....

164

1:30 AM Saturday Morning

TRAPPED IN
THE FORBIDDEN TUNNEL

The sudden blast of light almost blinded Andrea as it poured out into the cavern. She thought something must have gone wrong with her lantern and lifted it higher to her face for closer inspection. It was then that everything fell into place. The voices. The light. Andrea had been caught!

She reacted instinctively, blowing out the lantern in one fast puff of air and diving to the ground. They hadn't spotted her. They were coming from the brightly lit basement of the building into the gloom of the cavern. Their eyes would need time to adjust. But it would only be a matter of minutes before they missed the lantern and realized that someone was in the for-

165

bidden tunnel. Andrea had to hide! She had a few minutes, maybe only seconds, to find a good hiding place. Even that was no guarantee that she wouldn't be discovered, but it was her only hope.

Andrea crawled frantically between the boxes and barrels, not worrying about making sounds. The men were making enough noise to cover any she might make. She wondered briefly what the men were doing coming out of that door. Did they have something to do with the big meeting that everyone seemed to be talking about? Andrea quickly pushed those thoughts aside. She had more important things to worry about right now, like where could she hide. Where would be a safe place? Suddenly it came to her, looming in front of her like a warm welcome hug. Without stopping to think about what she was doing, Andrea crawled into one of the barrels that was on its side in the dirt just as she heard a shout. "Hey! Where's that lantern gone?!"

Several pairs of feet seemed to shuffle noisily in the dirt and gravel. "It's a good thing we were sent out here to get more booze. Maybe we'd better take a look around. I think we got us a captive audience!" There was a smattering of laughter.

"Aw-w-w, ain't nobody here," another voice whined. "Let's just get that booze and get back inside. I don't want ta miss anything!"

"You'll stay put and stake this place out if ya know what's good fer ya," the first voice commanded. Soft curses were uttered. They grew more faint until total silence enveloped the area. The large cavern became a noiseless tomb. It was so quiet Andrea could hear her heart thumping loudly in her chest. It seemed to bounce and thunder against the wood of the barrel where she lay. Was anyone still out there, she wondered breathlessly. Could they hear her heart pounding? She prayed not.

Whispered voices and small scuffling sounds wafted through the inky blackness on moth wings. The men had obviously decided that someone was hiding and they began to search. Andrea wondered if her hiding spot was good enough. What could she do to make it better? Anyone with a light could shine it in and find her hiding. It would only be a matter of minutes. How could she tip the odds in her favour?

Andrea racked her brain as the sounds continued. What could she do? Of course! Moving carefully to the barrel opening, Andrea stuck her head out cautiously and peered around. She could see small lights moving in and around the heaps of boxes. What were they using, candles? She didn't know, nor did she really care at this point. But she was glad – weak light gave her an advantage, especially with her plan. She felt frantically around the barrel entrance. Lying beside the barrel Andrea discovered what she needed and dragged it over as quietly as she could. It was a broken old box. She stuffed it part way into the barrel, pulling it on top of her head and shoulders, and squeezed her body down further inside. If anyone shone a light on the barrel, all that would most likely be seen was a broken box. That wouldn't warrant any further investigation. At least that's what Andrea hoped. She whispered a small prayer of help and settled into her hiding place, her heart still thumping loudly in her ears.

There was a loud clank. Andrea jumped, hitting the box with her head. "I've found it!" a voice rang out. The lost lantern was relit and held high. Andrea could see it casting shadows about as it was danced around in the hope of throwing light on some poor desperate person.

"Sh-h-h, I'm sure someone's hidin' in here." The voice was strong and certain and all grew as quiet as a graveyard at midnight.

The silence was oppressive. It filled Andrea's ears and her mind until she thought she was going crazy. It pressed down upon her until she was sure that she could hear the blood moving through her veins. The very idea disgusted her completely and Andrea drew a slow soothing breath of stale air and let it out quietly.

"The kid musta taken down the lantern," someone muttered, breaking the silence.

"Naw, not him. He was hurtin' real bad when we left 'im. Someone else musta helped him."

"Just hang the light back up," a gruff voice ordered. "That way if someone is hiding here, we'll catch 'im as he goes past the lanterns. We'll get ya, sucker! We got longer stayin' power than you!" It was a threat and Andrea shivered. They knew she was there! She heard the clang of the lantern falling against the pole as someone hung it up and then all grew silent and stayed dead as a morgue.

For at least twenty minutes no one moved. No one even dared breathe aloud, but the men were still out there. Andrea could hear the odd shuffle once in a while. Suddenly she heard the soft whisper of words. The secret door must have swung open because light briefly flooded into the cavern and then disappeared, shut in behind the wooden door. All was left in blackness.

So, how many men had there been? And how many were left hiding in the cavern and tunnel waiting for Andrea to make her move? Andrea listened until she could hear the silence reverberating on her eardrums. She was going mad! How long could she wait in the cramped and damp, fermented smelling barrel while time ticked by slowly on invisible hands?

Andrea willed herself to lie still. She must stay calm. She must outwait them, it was her only hope. She began doing the relaxation exercises she had seen her mother use. She squeezed one fist and arm tight and held it for a few seconds and then released it. Slowly, with deliberation, she squeezed and released all of the muscles she could think of, one after the other until she felt at ease. In the process, her brain relaxed too and Andrea felt herself sink into a drowsy state as her eyes slid shut….

How long she slumbered, Andrea would never know. Suddenly she was shaken from her relaxed state by the crunching sound of gravel nearby. She opened her eyes just in time to see faint light pass by the opening of the barrel.

Andrea's heart kicked into overtime. It pounded double and triple time, sending adrenalin swooshing through her body, tensing every muscle. A pair of black-and-white patent leather shoes moved stealthily by the barrel within centimetres of Andrea. She could have reached out to touch them, had she so desired. They were still looking for her and waiting for her. She listened to the sound of the footsteps quietly fade away, taking the weak light too.

She couldn't stay here much longer, Andrea decided. She had to find a way out. To wait was foolhardy. They would eventually discover her, and then what? Andrea did not want to be around to find out. She needed to escape, but how? There were so many obstacles in her path; boxes, barrels, and bottles which she could barely see, no light to speak of, and men hiding, waiting for her. Did she have any advantages over them? Any shred of a plan that might work in her favour?

Yes. She did have one advantage. She knew where she was and they didn't! She didn't know if it was much of an advantage, but it was something. Now, if only she could figure out where they were and how many of them were out there. Andrea moved slowly and carefully into a sitting position in the barrel, taking pains not to scrape the sides of her hiding spot. Surely any sound that she made would capture their attention and bring them closer to discovering her.

From her sitting position Andrea gently and soundlessly moved the box that she had pulled over the entrance of the barrel. That gave her a wider view of the blackness around the tunnel. She could just make out the various stacks of boxes near her. Now, if she could figure out where the men were. Andrea searched the area but could see nothing. Then she smelled it. Was it possible? She sniffed again. Cigar smoke was beginning to permeate the cavern. Someone was smoking cigars. Ordinarily Andrea hated the smell of smoke, but right now it was love at first sniff. This might be another advantage for her.

Andrea sat up straighter, sniffing the air, her eyes roving and squinting. She wasn't even sure what she was looking for, until she found it. There, where she knew the three short steps and the secret door to be, was a faint red glow. Andrea watched it for several minutes, trying to observe a pattern of behavior. Every minute or so the pale red spot raised up a few centimetres and glowed brighter red for a few seconds. It was then lowered back to its original place. Here was the pattern Andrea was looking for! She knew where this guy was! Was he the only one? She didn't know. But at least she knew where one man was.

A plan was beginning to form in Andrea's excited mind. That man was guarding the door. That was all right with Andrea. She had no desire to go that way. In fact, she needed to go in the opposite direction to get back to the tunnel and Rosie's house.

Andrea's plan was to keep that man in sight as much as possible and slide from one stack of boxes to the next until she was as close to the tunnel and the pole with the relit lantern as she could get. She would reassess the situation from there and come up with the second part of her plan, if she didn't get caught. It was pretty risky, but she really had no choice. Obviously, that man wasn't going anywhere anytime soon. She still didn't know if he was alone, but she could see a little bit. Hopefully she could sneak quietly along, keeping a sharp lookout for any of the others who might be waiting for her somewhere nearby.

That plan in place, Andrea took a deep steadying breath and cautiously eased her cramped body out of the barrel. It rocked a tiny bit and Andrea froze, half in, half out, holding her breath. Good, no noise. She could just see the faint red glow of the cigar some metres away over the edge of a stack of boxes. Obviously the man was in the same place. So far, so good.

Andrea crawled the rest of the way out of the barrel and waited, crouched beside it, listening and looking. She could see the faint outline of a stack of boxes a few metres ahead and away from the glowing cigar end. Andrea carefully got down on all fours. The bulge of coins clinked gently in her pocket and she froze, petrified that she would be caught. She glanced quickly back to see the red glow of the cigar still smouldering and felt the air swoosh out of her lungs in relief. He must be slightly deaf, Andrea thought, but she knew she had to do something. She couldn't have the coins jingling as she moved. What could she do? Did she have anything she could stuff in her pocket? Andrea shook her head trying to kick-start her brain. Vance's cap jiggled and threatened to fall off. Of course. The cap! Andrea swiftly removed it and stuffed it into her already bursting pocket. It just barely fit, but it held the coins trapped and tight. They had no room to clink and rattle one against the other. Great! Luck seemed to be on her side so far.

Andrea reached the first stack of boxes and snuck around behind them. There she rested, cautiously stretching her arms and legs to get the kinks out. It had been difficult to stay in one cramped position for so long and her muscles were complaining about it. Andrea placed her hand against the cloth of her pocket and the bulge of coins and stretched up. Looking back, she could still see the tiny glow of the cigar, although it was getting fainter the further away she got.

Andrea peered around the other side of the boxes looking toward the tunnel entrance. She couldn't see it yet, but the faint glow of the lantern told her where it was located. She spotted another stack of boxes and quietly set out on hands and knees toward it.

Andrea proceeded in this fashion, from one stack of boxes to another, for several minutes. Each time she reached her destination, she looked back to find the red glow of the cigar getting smaller and smaller, but still in the same place. Ahead, the light from the lantern began to brighten as she moved closer, putting her more and more at risk of being seen the closer she got to the pole.

At last Andrea reached the very last stack of boxes. Nothing now stood between her and the tunnel except the lighted lanterns. She paused to rest awhile and to think of a plan. The lanterns with their weak light – the very things she had depended on for security all night – were now her foes. They seemed doubly bright, giving off so much light that Andrea was sure that she could have read a paperback by the light filtering in around her hideout. She was not safe here, she realized. The light would give her away in no time. The sooner she thought of a plan, and acted on it, the better. But what plan? Andrea huddled beside the boxes in the dark shadows and searched her brain. How could she get away safely?

Of course! She would run. She would run straight out the tunnel and up to Rosie's place. But how could she make sure to give herself enough of a head start so that the men would have trouble following her? She squeezed her eyes shut, thinking of all of the action and adventure movies her brother was so fond of. What would some of those movie characters do in a situation like this?

Yes! Andrea smiled. It was all so simple. She really should have thought of it long ago. It would work, it had to work. It was her only hope. Andrea ran her hand along the earthen floor. She tested the weights of and discarded several items before choosing the one she thought would work the best. This was it! A piece of wood broken from one of the boxes. It would make the loudest noise and it wasn't too heavy. Andrea was sure she would be able to throw it quite far away from where she was actually hiding. Hopefully, it would make a loud bang, distracting the men. They would run toward the sound and Andrea would run in the opposite direction. Andrea had seen it done enough times in the movies to trust that it would work. Still, she was afraid. What if –? But no! She wouldn't think about that.

Not giving herself time to think or to worry, Andrea carefully stood up and heaved the heavy piece of broken box as far as she could in the opposite direction than the one she intended to travel. It landed with a loud thud that sounded like a sonic boom after the oppressive silence. Andrea watched from her spot as three figures came unglued from the shadows, each running in the direction of the sound. They were shouting advice to one another. One ran past so close that Andrea could have easily hit him with a stick. She let him hurry by unencumbered, counted to three, just to make sure that he was far enough away, and took off in the opposite direction through the forbidden tunnel, coins thumping against her leg with every step.

Andrea ran like the wind, feeling as if the devil was on her heels. She wouldn't fool the men for long, she knew that. She just needed enough of a head start to get safely into Rosie's apartment before they caught up to her. She could hear their voices and sounds of boxes being thrown. Good, they were still busy looking for her, that would give her more time.

In the murky light, Andrea tripped over something. She felt her left ankle twist painfully. "Ouch," she muttered, trying to ignore the pain. She swiftly got to her feet and took a few tentative steps. Her ankle throbbed with pain. The coins didn't help either. They were heavier than Andrea expected. It was like having a pocket full of toonies. They weighed down heavily on her left leg, causing her ankle to hurt even more. Andrea knew she couldn't hesitate for too long, the men would spot her soon enough. Glancing up she realized in panic that she still had a long way to go. She pressed bravely on, running with a limp, favouring her sore joint.

The run was tiring and very terrifying. Her lungs felt as if they were going to explode! Her chest hurt and her side ached, as well as her ankle. She wondered if anyone's heart had ever burst from fright and overexertion. Still Andrea pushed on in the dank tunnel, running faster and harder than she ever had.

Andrea knew the second the men realized that she wasn't there. She heard loud curses and the sound of the lantern being whipped from its peg on the pole. She ran faster, listening to the sounds of running steps behind her. They were gaining!

At last, when Andrea was positive that she could not run another step, she saw the wall ahead. It looked like the same dead end and for a second Andrea was startled. She had forgotten about the secret door. Where was it!? She searched, her eyes scanning back and forth as she approached the wall. She wouldn't have time to stop and look for it and there was no where else to hide if she couldn't find it. It was a one-shot deal. She had to get it right.

There it was! The door appeared faintly in the earth. Andrea thought it must be a figment of her exhausted imagination. She had heard of mirages before, the kind that appear just as the person is about to die. That would be just her luck. Not taking a chance, Andrea pushed on the secret door with all her might. It flew open, banging into the wall on the other side. Andrea jumped through the doorway landing on her tender ankle. She winced as she quickly shut the door tightly. Maybe that would slow them down a bit.

She was now in the narrow winding tunnel. It was shorter, but the twisting turns caused her to slow down and she lost precious seconds. The men were almost breathing down her neck! She heard the first door bang open again as she reached the next one. She fell through it, shutting it quickly.

Andrea stumbled up the stairs and reached her hands over her head to push open the heavy cellar door. This was the clincher. Andrea wasn't sure that she could budge it. It was so large and heavy and she was almost totally spent physically. What if she couldn't get the door open? What a place to die, Andrea thought, her chest heaving.

No way! Not now, not here! She took a huge breath and pushed on the cellar door using her arms, head, shoulders, and back. It moved! Andrea squirmed out and let the door bang shut. She glanced quickly up at Rosie's third floor window, gulping the night air. A figure was watching for her. Rosie.

"Turn off the lights!" Andrea tried not to yell. It was very late at night and she didn't want to wake the neighbours. Besides, the fewer people to witness her escape the better. You just never knew whose side anyone was on in this town. "I'm coming up!" Andrea continued. "Open the door!"

She could hear the men as they burst through the second door. It was only a matter of seconds before they would be standing right where she was. Andrea took off around the side of the house, stumbling on her aching ankle. She jumped the stairs three at a time, gritting her teeth to help ease the pain. Throwing open the screen and inner doors, she ran through, pausing just long enough to make sure she closed them again. No sense in giving the bad guys any clues as to where she might be. She then dashed up the inner stairs three and four at a time. She slid into Rosie's dark kitchen and collapsed on the floor in a breathless heap of sweat and grime.

Rosie quickly shut the door behind her and locked it. She motioned for Andrea to be quiet. With her breath coming in huge gulps, it was difficult. Andrea willed herself to calm down. She was safe now, at least for a while. She edged closer to the window, which was open, and peered out through the thin white curtains. There, she saw three men standing beside the open cellar door looking in all directions. "We need to find him!" A voice carried up and into the silent kitchen.

"But who, boss? We don't even know who we're lookin' fer. Nobody got a good look at'im."

"Just find him!"

Rosie gasped. "Al!" she moaned into trembling fingers. "Why you dirty, double-crossin' snake." Her eyes glittered dangerously as she spat the words quietly into the air. "He didn't leave town after all! He lied to me." She whirled around facing Andrea, her fists clenched, looking for answers.

Andrea waved Rosie away as Vance patted her shoulder. "Later," Andrea whispered, frantic to keep them quiet. "We'll talk about him later."

The three watched from behind the curtain as the men fanned out looking for Andrea. Several times they glanced up at the house, but each time they shook their heads. Every light was out; the place was silent as a tomb. Everyone was obviously sleeping.

The three in the window watched silently from behind the curtain as the men on the ground conducted their search. They looked under bushes and kicked at fences, peered into outhouses hoping to scare the runner out. After fifteen minutes they gave up, converging again beneath Rosie's still black window. "No luck, boss." One of the men needlessly reported.

"I can see that!" Al retorted angrily.

"How could we lose him?! We weren't that far behind him!"

"He sure could run fast!"

"Faster than you morons," Al said angrily.

Andrea choked back laughter behind her fingers when she heard that comment, her head swinging toward Vance. She shrugged her shoulders. "I'll tell you all about it later," she whispered with a smile. Vance gave her a salute with his good hand and grinned back faintly. He looked so pale that Andrea was afraid he would pass out and slide off the chair.

The men's voices grew fainter as they walked around the side of the house. Andrea panicked, grabbing Rosie's shoulder in a tight squeeze. "They're coming!" she whispered. "Quick! Hide me!"

"Ouch!" Rosie slapped Andrea's hand away. "They ain't comin'. They're going across the street to play cards and drink all night."

"You're sure?" Andrea asked doubtfully.

"Sure, I'm sure. I've been living here for a long time. You're safe now." Andrea still looked dubious, so Rosie grabbed her hand. "Come on, I'll prove it to you." She led Andrea out of the kitchen and down a narrow hallway to a door. Rosie pushed the door open and directed Andrea past a neatly made narrow bed and over to the window which faced the street. They peered out just in time to see the men disappear into the house directly across the street. A bright light flashed on in the living room window as a hand hastily drew heavy drapes across the large window. "See there. They're gone."

Andrea turned away from the window and gave a huge sigh of relief. She followed Rosie back into the tiny kitchen and plopped down into a chair. The jangling of the coins reminded her of her successful mission and she reached into her pocket. She pulled out the cap and laid it on the table and then pulled out the coins.

"Here's your money, Vance," she reported, dropping the twenty-one coins into his outstretched hand, dirt and all.

Vance weighed the money in his palm before awkwardly slipping it into his pants pocket. It was easy to see that he was in great pain. His actions were slow and deliberate, as if he were trying to minimize his movements. "I'm sorry," he finally apologized through clenched teeth.

"What for?" Andrea was puzzled.

"I realized once you left that I probably only had eighteen coins. And after what Rosie said, I thought you might be afraid to come back, or else ya spent lots of time lookin'. It was that blow ta the head," he explained, rubbing the goose egg above his left eye. "It's left me dazed and a little addled."

"What?!" Andrea stared at Vance dumbfounded. "Now you tell me," she thundered. "And I risked my life! Almost got caught! I got chased like a hunted animal! All for three lousy coins!" She took a deep breath to try and calm down, but it didn't work.

"Do you know what I went through to get those coins? Do you know how close I came to getting caught? Do you know where I found 'em?!" She was ranting now. It must be a form of stress release, she thought. Andrea ran agitated fingers through her tangled hair, feeling a fine shower of dirt rain down upon her shoulders. She glanced over at Vance, condemning words dying on her lips. He sat, head back against the hard wooden chair, eyes closed, looking for all the world as if he'd fainted.

"Rosie? Come quick!"

Rosie came hurrying across the kitchen with a cool glass of lemonade for Andrea. "Drink this," she said soothingly, "I'll take care of Vance." She patted his shoulder and rinsed a cloth in a basin of water on the table nearby before pressing it against his forehead.

Rosie glanced at Andrea's face, really studying her for the first time since she had returned with the coins. "You are a filthy mess," she declared. Another cloth was lying on the table. Rosie rinsed it out and passed it over to Andrea. "Your face is so dirty your own mother wouldn't even recognize you! Go on," she urged gently when Andrea didn't immediately take the cloth. "Wash up. You'll feel better."

Andrea took it, wondering at Rosie's sudden change of heart. Perhaps Rosie now saw Andrea as someone to be trusted, since she had returned with all the money. Smiling tiredly to herself, Andrea set to work, doing the best she could with the washcloth and basin of water. Rosie placed a small mirror on the table. Andrea held it up to study her features. Rosie was right. Dirt and grime were smeared on her cheeks and across her nose. Sweat appeared to have mixed with the dust on her forehead, creating a slimy mess of caked mud. Andrea chuckled as she scrubbed at her face. She couldn't ever remember being this dirty. If only she had a camera. She would love to get a snapshot of her face. She looked like an owl, large round eyes peeking out from the grit and mud.

"There, now, tell us the whole story," Rosie suggested as Andrea finished drying her face on a white towel. She had to admit that it did feel clean and cool, although a nice hot shower would have felt much better.

Rosie took the basin to the sink and replaced it with cool clear water. She settled herself into the chair across from Andrea. "Don't leave anything out, especially the part about Big Al the Snake Face still being in town," she said as she placed her elbows on the table, giving Andrea her full attention. She glanced curiously at Andrea.

"Glad ya didn't lose that cap," Rosie commented suddenly, swiftly leaning to the side to block Vance's view. Her eyes darted sharply from the cap to Andrea's head and back again. With a soft gasp, Andrea grabbed the cap from the table, where she had put it. She slammed it on her head with a sigh of relief. Vance still didn't know her real identity and now was not the time for true confessions. She smiled her thanks at Rosie and sipped the refreshing lemonade. It tasted wonderful to her parched dry throat.

Between sips of lemonade, Andrea told her story, leaving nothing out. At times her audience looked skeptical. Once they actually told her to quit exaggerating! As Andrea looked back on it, she realized just how unbelievable it all seemed. She almost didn't believe it herself, except that she had the scrapes and scratches to prove it. "I guess those men came out of that door into the storage area to get more liquor. They sure scared the socks off me! I almost fainted from fright when I realized what was happening."

"Well, we're glad ya didn't get caught, Andy," Rosie smiled, patting Andrea's shoulder. "Real glad."

"Yeah, me too." Andrea sighed and tried not to think about what might have happened to her if she had been discovered trespassing in the storage area.

As the story came to the end, Andrea noticed that Vance was falling asleep in his chair. His head nodded from side to side and his body had shifted so that it almost slid to the floor. "Better take him home, girl," Rosie whispered softly.

Andrea turned her head quickly, anxiety filling her eyes. "He doesn't know." She nodded in Vance's direction.

"I know," Rosie stated. "And you'd like to keep it that way for now. He'd probably feel double-crossed to discover you're female." Andrea nodded and Rosie was silent for a few moments. "You haven't told me about Al yet."

"Oh, him." Andrea sighed. "I just didn't want to hurt your feelings."

"It ain't you hurting my feelings, girl, just tell it to me straight."

Andrea nodded sympathetically and told Rosie about Big Al's about-face in the tunnel and how he'd returned to the Hazleton instead of going to the train station as planned.

"Did he meet a woman there?"

Andrea jumped, her eyes dropping to the floor. She had hoped to avoid that topic specifically, but things were getting out of hand. She hated to be the one to break Rosie's heart. But Rosie wanted nothing but the truth. She glared at Andrea with ice cold eyes until Andrea caved in. "Yes, he did," she admitted softly.

"Who?"

"I really don't know. I didn't get a look at her, the light –" Andrea was stopped by the piercing glare of Rosie's eyes. Would she ever get on the good side of this woman, she wondered. None of this was even her fault and yet she felt like somehow it must be. "It's her voice I remember," Andrea reluctantly revealed. "Low and – and soft, like honey on toast."

"Susie!" Rosie growled. "That no good simpering baby face with her bedroom voice! She was always after my man!"

Suddenly Andrea was angry. She stood bracing her hands on her hips. "He's not worth the effort, Rosie," she snapped, glaring down at her. "You can do much better than that. He's a jerk! A two-timing idiot who didn't know a good thing when he had it. He thinks friends are garbage and not worth having. He says that they can't be trusted, but it's him you can't trust! He's not worth crying over, Rosie, believe me!"

"Well, well, well," Rosie eyed Andrea, a look of respect on her face. "So you do have a backbone."

"I have more than that! I have friends and I treat my friends well! I risked my life for Vance more than once tonight! That's what friends do!"

"Yeah, girl," Rosie smiled. "You're right. You're right about all of it. He is a two-timing piece of garbage. He's not worth the trouble and maybe I can do better than that. And," Rosie stuck her hand out to shake Andrea's, "I'd be proud to call you my friend. It doesn't really matter much where you're from. Even if you are a wee bit strange, still it's nice to have ya on our side."

Andrea shook the outstretched hand, a smile on her face. "Put 'er there, friend!"

Feeling as if she did indeed have two good friends, Andrea prepared to help get Vance home. Rosie directed her back to Main Street, warning them both to be very careful crossing it at this time of night. "It'll be deserted," she told them. "Any kind of movement will be noticed. Make good and sure that no one sees you, mind. Not Al's men and not the cops. Once you cross Main, walk one block further east to the park. It's not much of a park right now, just a large grassy place, mainly. But someday I'm sure it'll be a big beautiful park. Vance lives in the big old boarding house across from the park. You really can't miss it, and Vance'll be there to help you."

"You think it's safe to go out the front door at this hour?" Andrea asked uncertainly. "Don't you think Al might have one of his men keeping an eye out for anything unusual?"

"Hmm-mmm," Rosie thought. "You could be right. But we have ways!" She opened her apartment door and started silently down the stairs. "Sh-h-h."

Vance and Andrea carefully followed Rosie down to the first floor where she tiptoed over to a closed door and reached for a key that was hidden on the ledge above. She inserted the key into the lock and turned slowly. The door swung open noiselessly on oiled hinges and the three moved into the dark apartment. It was identical to Rosie's apartment, two floors above. "My girlfriend lives here," Rosie informed them, walking over to the open window. She pushed back the sheer curtains. "We've often used this means of entering and exiting the house. Come on, I'll lower ya to the ground."

Andrea went first, slipping over the window ledge and dropping lightly to the ground. It was only a metre drop but she landed on her feet beside the large cellar doors with a grunt of pain. She had forgotten about her sore ankle.

Getting Vance out of the window and to the ground was a difficult procedure. He gritted his teeth and cradled his wounded arm, sitting in the window. "How do I get down from here?" he ground out.

"Jump," Rosie directed.

"Jump!?" He shook his head defiantly. "It would hurt too much."

"I'll catch you," Andrea promised. She opened her arms, staring up at the huge lump Vance made sitting in the window. She knew she really couldn't catch him, but she could cushion his fall. "Come on, Vance. Someone's going to see you if you don't move soon."

He closed his eyes and gently slid his bottom forward letting gravity do its thing. He fell to the ground, toward Andrea's outstretched arms. She broke his fall with a grunt as they both fell to their knees. "You okay?" Andrea asked breathlessly, gently helping Vance to his feet.

"Yeah," Vance replied. "My arm's hurtin' like the devil though." He carefully adjusted his wounded arm. "My head's poundin' too. Let's go home."

With a quick wave to Rosie, Vance and Andrea headed off down the darkened yard, cutting over to the next street. All of the windows in the houses were black, but open to catch the night breeze. Curtains swayed gently from their hooks.

The short jaunt to Main Street was uneventful and even peaceful. But crossing Main might present problems. Andrea thought about it as they walked along. She decided that she would park Vance in the shadows of the large building on the corner and then sneak out to have a good long look. They would then hurry as fast as possible across the street and into the dark shadows on the other side.

Luckily, Main Street was deserted. Andrea had never seen a more desolate sight. It looked like something out of a movie about the end of the world. All of the buildings silent and dark and no people around. Only a few street lights still twinkled and gleamed brightly against the pitch black sky. Andrea wondered briefly where the moon was. She scanned the black void above and decided that it must be a new moon; that would help explain the welcome darkness that enveloped them as they hurried on.

During the endless walk through the large park, Andrea allowed herself to feel lonely. She hadn't thought about her family in hours and now she found herself really missing them. She felt tears prickle in the back of her throat. Her nose got stuffy and her eyes began to water. What would Vance think if she suddenly put her head down and cried, wailed like a baby? That's what she felt like doing, but she knew that she couldn't allow herself the luxury at the moment. She had a job to do.

She had to get Vance home safe and sound.

Andrea looked at him trudging along beside her, clutching his arm. He weaved now and then, looking as if he would collapse before taking the next step. Andrea put a protective arm around him and he leaned into her. "There's my house," he finally reported when Andrea was sure that she couldn't take another step. She was now supporting both Vance's weight and her own. They were directly across the street from a large rambling house with a big wraparound veranda. There was a sign neatly printed and nailed on the little white fence in front. "Viola's Boarding House."

"My mom runs the house and I try ta make extra money in the tunnels," Vance supplied. "I did real well tonight, thanks ta you." He gave Andrea a weak smile that couldn't conceal his pain-filled eyes.

"You really need to see a doctor, Vance." Andrea was getting more concerned about him by the minute.

"Let's see what Mom says. She's pretty good at doctorin' herself. Had ta do it enough times."

They hobbled up the front steps, the weight of the night suddenly heavy on their bodies. Viola met them at the door. "Oh Vance!" she whispered, gently but firmly pushing Andrea away and helping Vance into the tidy living room. She led him over to the well-worn sofa where he collapsed in a heap. Andrea followed behind and stood in a corner out of the way while Viola quickly got water in a basin, cloths, and brown glass bottles that contained smelly medicines. She doctored Vance on the sofa, examining his arm and bathing his cuts and swollen eye.

"I knew this would happen," she muttered to herself as she worked. "How many times have I asked you – begged you – to quit hanging around those tunnels?!"

"Aw, Ma," Vance groaned, "you know I can't just quit. We've talked about this before. It doesn't work that way. He'd come lookin' for me. I know too much about the business. Though it looks like I'm on the outs now. Let's just hope he leaves us all alone."

"Well, I'm going to send for Doc Anderson first thing in the morning. We need to see how badly you're hurt. I'd send for him now, but I know he's out on another call. I saw him go high-tailing out of town this afternoon. Apparently Mrs. Jackson is having trouble birthing her baby…." Her voice trailed off as she bent to kiss her son's bruised cheek.

"You can doctor me, Ma, you always have, and Andy and Rosie fixed me up pretty good." Vance tried to sound tough, but his voice quivered as his eyes slid shut.

His mother sighed audibly. "Oh, Vance, you do try a mother's patience."

Vance nodded, his eyes still closed, gritting his teeth against the pain.

2:10 AM Saturday Morning

INTRODUCING BEANIE

"Hello."

A small tired voice made Andrea jump. She whirled around to see a tiny girl dressed in a white night-gown standing nearby in the entrance to the living room.

"What happened to Vance?!"

Andrea didn't know what to say. How much did Vance's family know about his nighttime activities? She was saved, though, for Viola turned around, suddenly becoming aware that Andrea was still there.

"Oh. I'd forgotten about you. I'm sorry. Thank you for bringing Vance home. He's going to be all right, Beanie."

Beanie, that must be the little girl's name, Andrea

decided. What a strange name. It must be a nick-name.

"But what happened to him?" the little girl demanded.

"He just got hurt wr-wrestling." Viola lied with difficulty, stumbling and stuttering over the words.

"You mean he got beat up!"

"Beanie! That's not what I said. Now, go back to bed."

"I want to know what happened!" The child placed her arms on her hips and glared at her mother. "You think I don't know! You think I don't know where Vance goes at night! Well I do! He goes into those tunnels and now he's beat up!"

"Where did you hear about the tunnels?" Viola left Vance's side and came to tower over Beanie, her voice dripping in anger.

Andrea gave the child credit, she stood her own ground, staring back at her mother. "Everyone knows about the tunnels, Ma," she said breezily, dramatically waving her hand in the air. "Why, Jane's brother —"

"That's enough!" Viola almost shouted. She took a breath and looked over at Andrea as if suddenly remembering her presence again. "We have company just now. We'll discuss this later."

She turned her attention to Andrea, putting her arm on her shoulder and escorting Andrea out of the living room and to the door. "Thank you again, for bringing

Vance home. We really do appreciate it." She studied Andrea's shocked face. "You do look familiar, but I don't know you, do I?"

Andrea shook her head, suddenly unable to talk. Vance's mother was kicking her out of the house! She had nowhere to go, no money for food, no place to sleep. Her throat clogged up with tears and she gulped hard. If she didn't get control and explain the situation, she'd be sleeping under a tree in the park soon, and that she did not want to do!

"Let her – I mean, let him stay for the night, Mom," Beanie advised.

"Pardon?" Viola looked from Andrea's distressed face to Beanie's willful one and back again.

"Sh – he looks hungry and tired. I bet he doesn't have a place to stay."

Viola looked closely at Andrea. "Is that true? You don't have a place to sleep tonight?" Andrea shook her head, tears so close that she could taste them. "Well, why didn't you say something, child?" Viola gently chided as she lead Andrea back into the house.

"You can sleep in Vance's bed, since he'll be using the couch tonight. I'm not one to turn away a person in need. Any friend of Vance's is a friend of the family. I'm sorry I didn't realize sooner. I-I should have guessed, but my mind's been preoccupied with Vance…." Her words petered out as she realized that

Beanie was still standing nearby. "What's your name, boy?" she asked.

Andrea cleared her throat loudly. "An-Andy," she croaked.

"Well, Andy. That's short for Andrew, I imagine. It's nice to meet you."

"Now, Beanie, please get the boy some clean sheets and warm water in a basin, and a towel. He needs to clean up a bit before falling into bed." Beanie ran off to do her errands, flashing a big bright smile at Andrea. When the child had disappeared down the long hallway, Viola asked, "What did happen to Vance tonight? I was getting very worried about him. He's usually not this late."

"He got beat up, ma'am." Andrea had never used that word before but somehow it seemed right.

"By Scarface and his men, I take it," Vance's mother supplied when Andrea didn't speak.

Andrea nodded. "Scarface got mad at him about something. I'm not sure what, exactly. But Scarface isn't a very nice man, I've discovered."

"I wish Vance didn't feel the need to go into those tunnels. It's so dangerous." Viola sighed and wrung her hands. "But the money is so good; too good to pass up. And it is so adventuresome and exciting... for young fellas like yourself. I know that he feels trapped by that terrible man. Do you really think Scarface would come looking for him if he quit?"

Andrea sighed and nodded. "I've come to understand the pull of that man too. It's a scary thing. You
think you owe him something, like trust or loyalty,
but it doesn't work both ways. He double-crosses you
or hurts you and doesn't even care, and then he still
expects you to be loyal to him. I think he might come
looking for Vance if he felt he had a reason to. But
since he already had him beat up tonight, I think he
might just forget about him."

"Your room's ready," Beanie announced from the
hallway. Both her mother and Andrea jumped, startled by her nearness. Andrea wondered just how long
she had been standing there listening.

"Good-night, Andy," Viola called softly as Andrea
followed Beanie down the hall. "Sleep well."

Vance's room was small and cramped but very
clean. It held one narrow bed and a small wooden
dresser with a mirror. The basin of warm water stood
on the dresser. The bed was freshly made with the
sheets turned back invitingly.

"How old are you?" Andrea asked Beanie. Anyone
who could talk to adults so convincingly and make a
bed so well couldn't be as young as she looked.

"Ten." The child announced. "What's your real
name?"

Andrea looked over her shoulder at the little girl.
She sat at the foot of the bed, her short chubby legs
pulled up under her nightgown. "How did you

guess?" Andrea asked. "Even Vance hasn't figured it out yet. And neither has your mom."

Beanie shrugged her shoulders in a childish way. "I just guessed. You kinda walk like a girl, I guess. And, I'm sorry to say, a fella probably wouldn't cry about having to sleep outside."

"Yeah, you're probably right," Andrea agreed. "Andrea is my name." She reached up and removed Vance's cap, running her fingers through her hair. It felt good to massage her scalp and loosen the dirt and gravel embedded there. Thank goodness Rosie had let her clean up a little bit, or she'd really look a sight. How she wished she could take a shower and stand under the hot spray for an hour at least! But the basin of water would have to do.

"So, Vance got beat up by those gangsters," Beanie muttered angrily. "I hate them! My friend Tommy's dad was found shot in the head, deader than dead, and everyone blamed Scarface, but no one ever found him! Isn't that terrible?"

"Yes, it's awful," Andrea agreed, shuddering with fear. It was hard for her to separate the fact from the fiction; to comprehend the reality of the danger she had been in, and was still in. If she had been caught tonight in the forbidden tunnel rescuing Vance, she would, at very least, be in as much pain as Vance from a severe beating. She might have even been killed. The thought spooked her and she shivered. "I'm sure the police are trying their best to catch him."

"Hmph," Beanie snorted, folding her arms on her knees. "I heard Tommy's uncle say that they're paid not to find him! Moose Jaw is so small, how hard could it be to find one man?"

Andrea raised her eyebrows. "What made you so worldly, girl?"

Beanie shrugged her shoulders, sighing in a dramatic way. "You can't live here and not see it; all the bad things happening, murders and robberies and strange men hiding in the dark. And I hate it. I worry every night that my big brother might end up like Tommy's dad...deader than dead."

"Well, there's nothing you and I can do about it," Andrea shrugged, turning back to her warm water. She squeezed out the washcloth and applied the soothing wetness to her scratched face. It felt good to take off another layer of grime.

"Vance does have a mind of his own. He can choose not to do it." She didn't mean for it to sound as glib and uncaring as it came out, but it did. She was truly exhausted. Her whole body was screaming to fall onto that clean, comfortable bed and sleep for about a million years.

Beanie jumped off the bed with a bump. "You're just like the rest of them," she spat. "You don't care about anything but the money you can make down there."

"That's not true," Andrea retorted, but she found

herself talking to the closed door. Beanie had exited the room, firmly closing the door behind her with a thump. Andrea stared at the back of the door, wondering if she should go after the child and present her point of view. She wondered again how Beanie could sound so grownup. She must have been listening to many adult conversations, discussing Big Al and his gang of criminals. Or maybe a child did grow up faster having to worry about her big brother's safety every night.

Andrea felt guilty for about three seconds and then the need to sleep took over. She shucked off her clothes as fast as possible, discovering that Beanie had left a nightshirt of Vance's on the bed for her. She shoved her head into the opening while crawling into bed. Pulling her arms through the sleeves, she dragged up the covers and laid her head on the pillow. She thought she might have trouble getting to sleep in a strange place, but no such problem occurred. As soon as her head hit the pillow, she was out like a light, in a deep, dreamless sleep.

ANDREA REMEMBERED NOTHING until the sound of Viola's voice dragged her reluctant mind into consciousness far too soon. She forced open her eyes; everything was engulfed in various shades of black. She'd only been asleep a few minutes by the look of it; it was still dark outside. Andrea tried to snuggle down into the bed, but

Viola's voice was anxious. "Beanie?" she called softly down the hall. "Beanie, where are you?!"

Beanie! Andrea jumped out of bed, a sense of doom and trepidation settling in the pit of her stomach. She tried to remember their last conversation before she'd gone to bed. Beanie had been upset and had stomped out of the room. Oh no! What was she up to? Andrea pulled open the bedroom door and discovered Viola hovering nearby, a frantic look on her face. "Is Beanie in there with you?" Not waiting for a reply, she pushed past Andrea to have a look for herself.

"No, she's not here." Andrea spoke to Viola's back-side, for she had bent down to peer under the bed. "I haven't seen her since I went to bed."

"Where can she be at this hour of the night?! I just went into her room to check on her before going to bed myself. Her bed hasn't even been slept in!"

A terrible thought began to grow in Andrea's mind. "You know," she spoke slowly, wondering if she should mention this to the child's mother or not. Andrea decided that she had better, considering that Beanie was definitely not at home and asleep as she should have been. "She was quite upset about Vance's getting beat up. And I think she overhead when I was telling you how it happened."

"She's gone after Ol' Scarface, I'd wager." Vance's voice was blurred and groggy.

"Vance!" Both Andrea and his mother rushed to

his side. "You should be resting!"

"I need to go after Beanie," he protested, fighting their hands away. He took two feeble steps and then fell heavily against the wall. He could barely stand up.

"I'll go after Beanie," Andrea decided instantly. "Just tell me where you think she is."

"Go back to Rosie's place. Rosie looks after Beanie sometimes for Ma when I can't. I think Beanie probably went there," Vance directed. "I'd go with you, but –"

"It's okay," Andrea told him, patting his shoulder. "Just stay here and keep your mother company. She must be worried out of her mind." Andrea hurried back down the hall to her room.

"Andy." Vance's voice sounded weak, but cheerful. "Make sure ya wear my cap. I can't believe how girl-like ya look, even in my nightshirt!" With a frail wave of his good hand he turned his head and shuffled back to the living room.

Viola eyed Andrea and shook her head. "You are a girl! And don't try to deny it. I was just as skinny and flat-chested as you at that age. I wonder why I didn't see it before! It's amazing that you've got Vance fooled, but I guess he'd never think that a girl would brave those dangerous tunnels. And that ridiculous haircut helps. You really should let it grow out a bit and put some pretty ribbons in it. Why would you want to look like a fella? And why are you working those tunnels?"

Andrea stood still, the white billowing nightshirt falling about her knees. "I – I –" She wanted to give Vance's mother an answer, to explain why she'd been trying to pass for a boy, but none seemed appropriate and she let the moment pass, shrugging her shoulders.

"I guess I better go find Beanie," she said by way of excuse, slipping around Viola and disappearing into the bedroom.

Andrea dressed as quickly as possible, pulling her filthy T-shirt and overalls back on. The bed looked so inviting, she would have given anything to be able to crawl back in and fall back to sleep. Jamming the cap back on her head, she hurried out of the room and headed to where Vance lay on the sofa.

"I still don't understand why Beanie would go to Rosie's," she stated flatly, as soon as she had rounded the corner. Viola was nowhere to be seen.

Vance motioned her closer and stretched up to talk softly in her ear. "I know Beanie," he started. "I betcha she's gone ta Rosie's ta get some help an' hatch some kinda plot against Big Al. Once Beanie gets hot 'n' bothered, she'll do anything. She's no namby-pamby, that one. She's a great ol' bean!" He was obviously proud of his little sister.

"But what could she possibly do?!"

"Well, I don't know, but I been talkin' her outta all sorts a schemes lately. She really don't like me workin' the tunnels, 'specially since –"

"Yeah, she told me," Andrea muttered, remembering.

"My gettin' busted up was probably the last straw for her."

"Oh boy," Andrea sighed. "I'll get over to Rosie's as quick as I can, then, and hope that she's there. Don't worry, Vance. I'll do my best to find her."

"Thanks." Vance grimaced as he lay back on the couch. "You're turnin' out ta be a much better friend than I thought ya would be. Ya sure saved my skin tanight."

"Well, that's what friends are for," Andrea said lightly, even though her chest threatened to puff out with pride. "We'll both be back soon, I promise."

"One more thing," Vance called as Andrea pulled open the front door. "Be careful. Stay outta sight!"

Andrea hit the street running and didn't stop until her lungs hurt and her legs felt rubbery. She sped through the night, through the park, and on toward Main Street. She knew she'd have to be quick. Dawn couldn't be far off, even though the sun was nowhere to be seen yet. The sky was as pitch black as a moonless night.

Crossing Main was no problem at all. Andrea stopped briefly to catch her breath, peering around the building to scan the road. It was as deserted as before, and she sprinted across and loped down the dirt path alley that would take her to Rosie's back window.

In the back yard behind the house, Andrea stopped short, gazing up at the vacant window. It was still open, the curtains fluttering gently in the light breeze. Andrea realized that she just couldn't go boldly around the front and climb the stairs. Who knew when the card games and drinking across the street would end? The bad guys might even be on their way over right now!

That awful thought galvanized Andrea into action. She could think of only one way to get Rosie's attention. If Beanie was up there, and Andrea sincerely hoped she was, then Rosie would be awake. Andrea searched the ground and quickly found what she was looking for – several small pebbles. Andrea aimed the first one at the window above. She wanted to hit the window or the side of the house with enough force to alert Rosie, but not disturb to the other tenants. She definitely did not want to break the window!

The first pebble made a soft ping against the house and fell to the ground. Andrea waited for a moment and then took aim with the second. It hit the window and bounced off. Andrea waited again. Nothing! How many pebbles would she have to throw? The third pebble disappeared right through the open window! Andrea stared wide-eyed. If it hadn't been such a serious situation, she would have laughed out loud. It was just like something out of a comedy show. Andrea bent down to search for more pebbles in the yard. Brother! This could take all night!

"Psst. Psst." Andrea looked up to see Rosie's sleepy face in the window. Her dishevelled hair stuck out in every direction.

"I need to come up," Andrea whispered. Rosie motioned to the same window below that Andrea and Vance had used earlier. Andrea nodded and stood waiting.

A short minute passed and Rosie's head reappeared in the lower window. She threw out a white knotted cloth, which hung down. "Grab this. I'll pull you up." Andrea did as she was told and soon found herself leaning half in, half out of the kitchen window. Rosie reached over her, pulling her legs in. She motioned Andrea to be quiet and then they quickly tiptoed out of the room and up the stairs to her own apartment.

"What's going on?!" Rosie demanded as soon as the door was closed. "Can't a body get any sleep around here?!"

"It's Beanie," Andrea quickly explained. "She's missing and Vance was sure that she'd be here. Have you seen her?"

"Tonight?!" Rosie asked, her voice full of surprise. "Of course not! I haven't seen her since –" She stopped short, a look of horror spreading across her attractive features. "No," she gasped. "She wouldn't have! Would she? Oh Beanie!" Rosie collapsed into the wooden chair beside the kitchen table.

"What?!" Andrea demanded. "Tell me!"

Rosie sighed deeply, running her fingers through her sleep-styled hair. "The last time I saw Beanie she was askin' me all sorts a questions about the tunnels. And I, stupid fool that I am, told her way too much. Oh dear. This is all my fault."

"Rosie!" Andrea interrupted her tirade. "It doesn't matter whose fault it is, we have to find her. If she's in the tunnels, we have to get her out, fast! There's no telling who and what is down there and it's almost morning!"

"You're right!" Rosie jumped up and ran to her bedroom, coming back in less than a minute in some semblance of dress. She grabbed a lantern from a shelf in the kitchen. "Let's go!"

"Where?" Andrea wanted to know. She didn't like the idea of just charging into the tunnels without a plan. "How are we going to get in? I don't think we should use the cellar entrance, do you?"

"Nope," Rosie said lightly. "Just have a little faith, girl, and follow me!" She led Andrea to the basement of the house.

"You have your own entrance?!"

Rosie laughed softly. "You bet I do. It's our little secret, mind. It was built when a 'business partner' of Al's bought the building. It's not used much anymore, now that the outside entrance has been added."

In the basement of the house stood the largest

armoire Andrea had ever seen. It had four large wooden drawers and a heavy mirror on top. Rosie set the lantern down nearby and lit it. It shed faint light around the room, casting large black shadows against the wall. There, leaning against the side of the bureau, in the shadows, was Beanie.

"Beanie?" Rosie spoke softly.

A faint sniff was heard and the small figure lifted its head. "Hey, Rosie. I couldn't move it," she sobbed, indicating the armoire she leaned against. "I couldn't move it, but I know there's an entrance behind it. You told me so!"

Rosie put her free hand on her hip and stared down at the child. "Just what do ya think you're doing here? Your mother is worried half to death about you."

Beanie stuck her chin out, staring at Rosie. "I don't care what you say. I'm going to stop Ol' Scarface and his men."

"And just what do you intend to do?"

"I-I don't know," Beanie replied with less certainty, "but there must be a way!"

Andrea joined Rosie at the armoire, staring down at the child. "There must be a way!" she repeated stubbornly. "He killed my friend's pa."

"You don't know that for sure," Rosie coaxed quietly. "Nobody knows for sure. Al is very careful about that sort of thing."

"I don't care. He was in on it. Why are you hiding him, Rosie? I thought you were my friend. I thought you cared about me and Vance."

"I do, honey, but it's not that simple. Everything's confusing."

"Not to me, it's not. Now, get outta my way. I have a job to do. If you're not going to help, then get lost. I don't need you around trying to confuse me, trying to get me to change my mind. Bad is bad, no matter how you look at it, Rosie. You can't cover it up and say it didn't happen, or he didn't do it. You just can't turn your back on a friend like that. That's like stabbin' him in the back." With that, stubborn Beanie put her head against her knees. "Now, go away. I'm trying to think of a plan."

Rosie took a step back, still trying to reason with Beanie. "This ain't a game, sweetie. It could be very dangerous. You could get caught. You are puttin' yourself, Vance, and your mother in danger. Not to mention me and Andy – the ones who came lookin' for ya."

"He had Vance beat up real bad. Vance could have been killed too, just like Tommy's papa. He's a mean man. Why do you like him so much?"

Andrea stood like a statue, listening to every word Beanie said. Out of the mouths of babes, she thought, remembering the expression she had heard her grandmother use. Now she knew what it meant too, she thought with wry amusement. Beanie made more sense than most adults. She was right! Killing and beating were terrible things. Why protect the people who did those things?

Each word Beanie spoke struck Andrea's very soul with a soft blow, causing a sensation of pain to settle in her chest. Her heart went out to Beanie, trying to do what she thought was right to avenge her friend's pain.

Andrea was embarrassed to admit that she had been conned by Big Al, for a short time anyway, while Beanie remained loyal to her friends. And Beanie knew the difference between right and wrong, too. Sometimes children saw things a lot more clearly than adults, Andrea concluded.

"Beanie," Andrea said, kneeling beside her, her mind made up. "I'll help you."

"Get some sense in your head, girl," Rosie admonished harshly. "You don't know what you're getting yourself into. She doesn't even have a plan!"

"Maybe not," Andrea smiled down into Beanie's worried face. "But I do. I know what we can do that will put us at little risk and it may make the police start investigating things around here."

"Yea!" Beanie cheered. She threw her arms awkwardly around Andrea's waist and squeezed. "You're a true blue friend!"

Andrea felt so good inside. Finally she was sure she was really doing the right thing, and it sure did feel great!

"What's the plan?" Beanie asked impatiently.

"First," Andrea said sternly, "you need to promise that you will never try to get into the tunnels again. It's no place for children and it is very dangerous."

"If you promise to help me now, I promise I won't try to sneak into the tunnels again. At least not until I'm big, like you!" Andrea sighed in exasperation, but didn't argue with the child. She knew that her plan would take some time and it was sure to start getting light outside soon.

Andrea nodded in agreement. "Okay. Second, you need to stay here, in the basement. I'm going to go into the tunnels. I'm leaving you in charge of this lantern. If you hear sounds that aren't from me, you blow this out and hide. Understand?"

Beanie nodded solemnly, as if suddenly realizing that this was not a game they were playing. "Now Rosie," Andrea turned to her, "are you in or out?" When Rosie remained silent, Andrea pleaded. "We really could use help right now, and Ol' Scarface sure hasn't been much of a friend to you tonight."

Rosie pursed her lips, thinking. "What if your plan fails? What if we get caught?"

Andrea shrugged her shoulders. "I'll do the most dangerous part, I – I don't really have a family to worry about." That wasn't exactly true, but Andrea didn't know quite how to explain it any other way. She really didn't have a family if she couldn't get back to the future.

"I'm in," Rosie said grimly. "I don't like it, but I'm not gonna let two little girls risk their lives. And you're right. Al isn't worth it!"

"Yea!" Beanie and Andrea both cheered softly. "Let's go then," Andrea said, remembering the time factor.

"But what's the plan?" Rosie wanted to know.

"I'll explain it on the way. It's really simple, actually. We just have to go down to that storage area where I was hidden for so long and pick up some empty bottles. It's not too far from here. Come on, Rosie, we haven't got all day."

It took both Rosie and Andrea, pushing and straining, to move the old armoire out of place. They entered the tunnel, standing for a few moments listening for others. Then, cautiously, they felt their way along. "I sure could use a flashlight," Andrea groaned without thinking.

"I don't know about any flashlight, girl, but we'll grab the first lantern we come to and take it with us." They entered the small winding tunnel and travelled along until they saw light beginning to appear. Rosie's tunnel joined up with the winding tunnel that lead to the cellar steps in Rosie's backyard. Andrea wasn't surprised that she hadn't seen the tunnel entrance before now. Both times she had used the tunnel, she had had a lot on her mind and this entrance was small and well camouflaged.

At the junction of Rosie's small tunnel stood a pole with a faintly burning lantern. It flickered frequently. "It's runnin' out of kerosene," Rosie stated grimly. "I sure hope it lasts." She grabbed it from the pole and they continued travelling as fast as they could while still being careful not to make much noise.

They didn't need to worry. The trip was fast and uneventful. In the tunnel, just where it widened into the underground cavern, Andrea motioned Rosie to hide. She then found a heavy stick and threw it into the stacks of boxes and barrels. It landed with a thump that caused them to jump, but no one else materialized and they knew they were truly alone in the dark.

Wasting no time, they each found a wooden box with empty liquor bottles and quickly carried it back up the narrow tunnel toward Rosie's place, remembering to replace the low-burning lantern on the hook as they went by.

"Well, did you do it?" Beanie asked excitedly when she saw them emerge from the tunnel.

"Not yet," Andrea reported as she and Rosie set their cases down and pushed the armoire back into place. Rosie quickly tidied the basement, removing all clues and traces of their visit. "We don't want to get any innocent people in trouble," she reminded them. "Now, what's the plan?"

"Well, it's a good one, but there is a small element of risk. We need to spread these bottles and the boxes on the road and on the steps and porch of the house where we last saw Big Al. The one right across the street."

"What?!" Rosie practically screamed. "That's a huge risk you're talkin' about. Just how do you think we can do that?! They may have a guard watching!"

"No, I don't think so," Andrea spoke confidently. She turned to where Beanie was jumping up and down in excitement. "How did you get into this house, Beanie?"

"I just walked up the front steps."

Rosie regarded her through narrowed eyes, not quite convinced. "Don't you think someone would have come to investigate if they'd seen her come here alone at this hour?" Andrea asked.

Rosie thought about it for a moment or two and then nodded.

"So, that's the plan. But it sure would be nice to have a disguise of sorts." Andrea said.

"A disguise?" she questioned. Andrea could hear a warm smile in her voice. "I may have just the thing." Rosie moved across the basement and pulled a box from a shelf against the wall. "I used this for Halloween last year. What do you think?" She held up a pair of striped overalls and a train engineer's cap.

"Perfect," Andrea smiled. "I'll do this part," she volunteered, figuring she had less to lose than the others if she got caught. They had family and friends here who could be hurt. Andrea was basically alone. That thought made her sad, but she pushed it away. Now was not the time to begin feeling sorry for herself. She moved swiftly, jumping into the costume, and turned to the others for inspection. "So, what do you think?"

"You need some stuffing," Beanie answered, eyeing her critically. "You need to look fatter."

Rosie hurried back to the box and pulled out a pillow. "Here, try this." She helped Andrea stuff it under the overalls. "Better?" she asked.

Beanie nodded. "Now what about your hair? If only we had a wig or something."

"We do!" Rosie exclaimed. She ran back to the box and pulled out a grey wig. "I used this for the town play, the year I played the witch in Hansel and Gretel." She plunked it on Andrea's head and readjusted the cap on top.

"There," she declared. "You're ready to go. We'd better hurry. It's going to get light soon. But if I know those men, they're asleep by now and will stay that way until mid-morning or longer. Still, we don't want to risk getting caught."

They quietly carried the cases of bottles upstairs to the big front door. "Now, you and Beanie need to be away from here," Andrea informed them. "Rosie, you go back to your apartment. Beanie, you sneak out of this door first and head for home now. Tell your mom that I'll be back soon."

"But –" both Rosie and Beanie tried to argue, but

Andrea wouldn't listen. "Look at how light the sky is getting. It'll be dawn soon, and people will be getting up. We need to do this fast and I don't want you two getting into trouble for it. Now go!"

Rosie nodded. "She's right, Bean." She gave Andrea a quick hug and headed up the stairs. "Keep the costume," she whispered as she went.

"Good luck," Beanie whispered softly. "This is a good plan, Andrea. And thanks for helping me. Watch out, though, and be careful!" With that bit of advice, she slipped out of the front door and disappeared into the greyness of the pre-dawn light.

Andrea took a deep breath and tried to calm down. Her heart thudded in her chest, sounding like thunder. She would need to have all of her wits about her if she was going to pull this off. She waited until she was sure that Beanie would be long gone and Rosie safe in her apartment, then she piled both cases of bottles into her arms and shuffled out the door.

Thank goodness the sun wasn't up yet and neither were the neighbours, as far as Andrea could tell. There were no lights shining from the windows in the nearby houses. The only sound was her shuffle as she trudged along under the weight of the heavy bottles.

Working quickly, Andrea spread bottles in the road and left one of the cases on its side. She wanted to make sure that it would attract as much attention as possible in the morning. Then she hunched down close to the ground and sneaked toward the house across the street from Rosie's, carrying the other case. She needed to plant the case and liquor bottles on the steps and porch of the house. She had to do it quietly so that no one would hear her.

Carefully, Andrea set the case down on the third step of the six leading up to the porch. She leaned into the steps and worked rapidly, spreading bottles this way and that. When the case was empty, she lifted it up and shoved it onto the porch. It made a scraping noise that caused her to freeze, staring at the door and windows above her. The house remained quiet and dark. Good. Andrea breathed again. She took the two last bottles and stood on the third step, reaching to place them on the porch. She set them down with a soft clink near the case and then turned and ran as if the very devil was on her tail.

Andrea ran hard, though it was awkward with the pillow bumping softly against her body with every step. She was overdressed and getting very hot. She slowed down, pausing only at Main Street to check for signs of activity. Nothing. She heaved a sigh of relief and hurried on. The costume! Andrea realized that she needed to ditch it. She couldn't be seen entering Vance's house in it. What should she do? Leaving it in the park wasn't a great idea either. It almost pointed a finger at Vance and his family.

Thinking hard, Andrea remembered that the

Hazleton Hotel was only a block away. She would ditch the costume there. That wouldn't lead to any one in particular, and, since Big Al stayed there, it might even point a finger at him! Behind the big hotel, she quickly pulled off the costume and tossed it in a heap beside the garbage can. She pulled the wig off last, and let it fall on top of the overalls. "Thanks costume, you made a great disguise."

The sky was now pinky-rose, though the city was still bathed in the pale light of very early dawn. If she ran, Andrea thought she could get back to Vance's before the sun actually rose over the buildings, announcing another bright sunny day. She took off at breakneck speed diagonally through the park, jumping the small creek easily and climbing its bank to the other side. She reached the edge of the park and stopped to catch her breath, walking almost casually up the front walk to Viola's Boarding House. Andrea covered her mouth as a huge yawn slipped out. She opened the screen door with her other hand and slipped quickly inside as the sun climbed into the morning sky.

A few blocks over, a newly appointed constable of the police force was just ending his night beat. As he walked down the quiet residential street toward Main, he spotted something lying in the road. On closer inspection, he knew that he had probably just come upon the lucky break that would lead to his promotion. To be able to catch the bootleggers and whiskey-mongers had been his dream since he had first set foot in Moose Jaw. His eyes sparkled with excitement as he trotted toward the police station to get extra help. He just knew it was going to be an exciting day!

5:45 AM Saturday Morning

TRUE CONFESSIONS

A ndrea's only thought was to check on Vance and then to fall into bed. She had pretty well been up all night and the lack of sleep and the great physical and emotional exertion was beginning to take its toll. She peeked into the living room, expecting to find Vance asleep. Instead he was sitting up, propped by pillows, awaiting her return.

"Andy!" he called excitedly waving her over with his good arm. "Tell me what happened! Beanie wouldn't say a thing. And Mom was fit to be tied! She dragged 'er down the hall by her ear. She won't be able ta sit down fer a week, I bet!"

Vance was much better. The colour had returned to

his face and the swelling had gone down. The bruises were still vibrant, though, around his injured eye.

"There's really nothing much to tell," Andrea said, exhaustion in her voice. "I found Beanie at Rosie's, just like you said, and sent her home. The rest can wait till later, I'm so tired I could sleep for a million years."

"Let Andy get some sleep now, Vance," Viola chided gently as she entered the living room. "You need to get some rest too. You've been nothing but a bundle of nerves since sh – ah – he left.

"Sleep as long as you need to, Andy," Vance's mother invited. "We are so grateful to you for going after Beanie like that and making sure that she got home safely. Our home is yours. You can stay here as long as you need to."

"Thank you." Andrea choked, tears forming in her eyes. She excused herself quickly, afraid that she might really cry in front of Vance and embarrass them all. She went down the hall to Vance's room and let herself in, closing the door softly behind her.

"Hey, Andrea," a familiar young voice greeted her.

Andrea jumped and then collapsed against the door. "Beanie," she admonished through clenched teeth. "Don't scare a person like that!"

"Sorry," Beanie muttered. "I just wanted to say thanks for helping me. You were brave, and I hope the trap works."

"Yeah," Andrea mumbled tiredly, "me too." She sat

down on the side of the bed near Beanie and leaned over to undo her Reeboks. They were filthy, caked with dirt and mud from the tunnels, grey with dust and grime. They would never be the same again.

"Those sure are strange looking shoes," Beanie commented, looking closely at them. "I've never seen such thick soles on shoes, and so white too! I don't think you're from around here, are you?"

"Nope." Andrea let her shoes plop down on the hardwood floor and removed her Mickey Mouse socks.

"Where did you get those socks?!" Beanie fingered the material. "It doesn't even feel like wool. My socks always make my feet itch. They're thick and usually lumpy. How can these be so soft and smooth?"

"It's synthetic," Andrea replied absently. She wiggled her damp toes, letting them air dry.

Beanie looked at her blankly. "Synthetic?"

"You know, it's made from man-made materials like polyester."

"Polly – what?!" Beanie studied Andrea very closely. "Something very strange is going on here. Just where are you from?" Beanie insisted.

"You wouldn't believe me if I told you, Beanie," Andrea sighed. "I hardly believe it myself." Andrea pulled her knees up and tucked them under her chin as she sat on the edge of the bed, thinking of her nice soft bed at home and the lovely warm shower she wished she was taking right this very minute. The movement caused the pockets in her overalls to bunch and something shiny slipped out and bounced onto the bedspread between the girls.

Beanie picked it up, fingering it. "A-n-d-r-e-a," she read slowly, turning it this way and that in the morning light. "What is this? It has your name on it."

"That's a barrette; a hair clip. I made it."

"You made this? It's really nice. C-can I have it?" she asked, suddenly shy.

"Sure," Andrea offered. "I have another one too, you can take them both, though this one has my last name on it." She leaned back onto the bed, digging into her pocket. "Here it is." She dropped the barrette into Beanie's eager fingers.

"T-a-l-b-o-t," Beanie read excitedly. "Hey! That's my last name too!"

"Really? Maybe we're related! Do you think we might be?"

"I guess maybe we could be," Beanie said vaguely. She was more interested in the barrettes. "How did you make these?" she asked, wonder in her voice. "You must be magic! Where did you get beads like that?"

"You can get them anywhere..." Andrea suddenly realized what she was saying, "...at least where I'm from," she finished quietly, knowing that she had been found out.

The room was very still as Beanie studied her for a moment. "Where *do* you come from, Andrea?" she demanded softly, an uneasy look settling on her face. "I have shivers running up and down my arms. Part of me feels like I should be scared of you, but I'm not. Where do you come from?"

Andrea sighed, partly in defeat and partly in relief. It would be good to talk to someone about it, even if Beanie was only a child. "I'm from the future," she sighed. "I hit my head on a mirror or something and I passed out. When I woke up, Vance was pulling me down one of the tunnels." The story spilled out of Andrea in a torrent. It was as if the floodgates had opened; she needed to talk to someone.

Beanie sat enthralled as she listened, her eyes big and round. "You don't believe me, do you?" Andrea finally slowed down and asked.

Beanie thought a moment and then nodded slowly. "That's just it. I do believe you. It all fits, you see, your strange clothes, these beautiful barrettes, and the different way you talk. It's like magic, like Peter Pan and Nevernever Land. I'm reading that book right now. You're like Peter Pan, well, you're more like Wendy, really. Wendy didn't belong in Nevernever Land and you don't belong here. But how will you get back?"

Andrea felt her throat close. She tried to swallow the lump. "I-I don't know," she mumbled quietly. "I don't know, and I really want to go home."

Beanie hugged her. "I hope you can find a way to get home. I wish I could help you. Vance has an old magic wand around here somewhere. Maybe we could practice magic spells!"

"Thanks," Andrea smiled through her tears, knowing that a child's magic wand wouldn't do the trick. Beanie was a puzzle to her. Sometimes she acted like a miniature adult and sometimes her childishness shone through.

"Maybe we'll meet again in the future!" Beanie suddenly bounced on the bed with excitement. "Let's see, in your life I'd be –" she quickly tried to count on her fingers and then gave up. "I just can't get the hang of numbers. My teacher sticks me in the corner almost everyday when we're doing our sums; I'm not very good at it. Anyway, I'd be an old lady for sure! I wonder what I'll be like?"

"Yeah," Andrea laughed weakly. "And I'd still be a kid. What would we ever have in common?"

"We'd have our adventure and our memories," Beanie told her firmly. "And besides that, we're related, remember?" She smiled. "Wouldn't that be enough?"

Andrea returned the smile, "Sure, Beanie. If – when I get back to the future, I'll look for you, but how will I recognize you?"

"Well," Beanie answered slowly. "I'll always have these." She opened her hand slowly. The sunlight coming through the window bounced off the barrettes, making them gleam. "I'll keep them forever," she vowed.

They said good-night to one another then, even

though it was fully morning. Birds chirped merrily in the trees outside their windows, but Andrea didn't hear a sound. She had fallen asleep even before her head hit the pillow.

Andrea stretched her arms over her head and sighed dreamily. She sat up pushing the blankets off and swung her feet over the edge of the bed. The strangeness of the room hit her as soon as her bare feet touched the cool hardwood floor. It should have been soft, plush carpet, if she was in her own room. She glanced around. There were no posters on the walls, her stuffed animals weren't sitting on the headboard, and her Walkman wasn't beside the bed. Nothing was right. Andrea wasn't back, safe and sound in her own room. She was still in Moose Jaw during the days of gangsters and Prohibition. It hadn't been a neat, but scary dream. It was reality, and that made Andrea tremble. A profound sense of loss and loneliness filled her soul. Would she ever find a way to get back to the future?

Andrea would have sat there for a lot longer if a timid knock hadn't sounded on her door. "Come in," she called out, half hoping to see her own mother poke her head around the corner. Instead an energetic look- ing Beanie leaned in. "Ma wondered if you're feelin' sickly. It's almost six o'clock," she reported. "And Ma says I'm to just wake you up and come right back, she doesn't want me bothering you."

"Six o'clock?!" Andrea scrambled off the bed, still wearing Vance's nightshirt. She grabbed her Mickey Mouse watch from the dresser. "I slept for twelve hours! Tell your mother that I'm getting dressed right now. I'll be out soon." Beanie nodded and went in search of her mother.

Andrea waited until the door whispered shut and then sprang into action. She looked around for her filthy overalls and T-shirt. She was sure that she had kicked them off and left them in a heap on the floor last night. She discovered them fresh and clean, neatly folded on the end of the bed.

It felt good to be getting dressed in clean clothes. Andrea hadn't relished the thought of putting on clothes that had been dragged through so much dirt, grime, and grit. She would have to remember to thank Mrs. Talbot. Andrea wondered again, as she pulled the sun-warmed T-shirt over her head, whether she was related to these Talbots in some way. She would have to remember to ask her Grandfather – if she ever got back home again. The seed of sadness nestled in her heart threatened to burst open. Andrea left the small bedroom and went in search of Vance. She needed a distraction to keep her mind off her lonely, aching heart.

The hallway and living room were deserted when Andrea went to investigate. She had expected to find

Vance still propped up on the couch. Instead she spied him through the living room window, sitting in the screened-in porch.

"Hi, Vance," she greeted as she stepped through the door. The afternoon sun shone hot and lazy across the painted floor boards.

"Hey, Andy!" Vance returned. He looked so much better, though his eye was still swollen shut and purple in colour. His wounded arm was encased in a sparkling white triangular bandage which held it in place on his chest. "I was beginning to think that you'd sleep all night too! And I've been so wantin' ta talk to you! Ma wouldn't let me wake ya up. She said you needed your sleep."

"Guess I was tired," Andrea said. "But how's your arm?"

"Oh," Vance moved it a little bit and winced. "It's still plenty sore. Ma already sent for Doc Anderson…." He let that thought slip away, worry lines etching his forehead. "But you certainly had quite an adventure last night," he said after a moment. "All kinds of excitement! Why don't ya sit here and tell me all about it now that you're all rested up." Vance leaned forward to pat the high-backed wooden chair beside the chaise longue on which he reclined.

"I should probably talk to your mother first to thank her for letting me stay here and all –" Andrea said pointing toward the door.

"You're more than welcome." Mrs. Talbot materialized with a tray of food. "I thought the two of you might be hungry. You can eat and visit. Our guest is probably famished."

"I am!" Andrea spoke, suddenly realizing how true it was. She couldn't remember the last time she had eaten.

Mrs. Talbot set the tray down on a small table near by. "Just help yourself, Andy, and if you wouldn't mind serving Vance?"

"Sure, no problem, Mrs. Talbot. I can do that."

Once they were settled, with plates of food and drink, Andrea told Vance of all of her adventures after she had left him. He listened, wide-eyed, almost as if he didn't believe her. He nodded here and there, chewing thoughtfully, when she came to the part about leaving the boxes and bottles on the porch.

"So, now what do ya think of Ol' Scarface?" Vance asked. "Some friend, eh?"

"He was never a friend, Vance," Andrea said. "I don't know how I got tricked like that. I'm sorry I got you beat up! You can't even go to work now."

"No," Vance sighed looking at his sore arm. "But it's probably better this way, and my ma's glad about it, in a way. She thinks its way too dangerous. It's just that we really do need the money –"

"Yeah," Andrea agreed. "Everybody needs money, especially around here."

Vance studied her through narrowed eyes. "You always say such strange things. Of course we need money! This boarding house is our only income now that I'm laid up."

Andrea noticed with interest that Vance's gangster accent was slowly fading from his speech. He was almost speaking like a normal person. Andrea thought the accent must be contagious. Perhaps when you hung around those guys you had to talk like them. She had even noticed that she had taken on the dialect once or twice during the evening.

"Maybe you could find another kind of job," Andrea offered. "There must be something else to do around here."

"I suppose so," Vance agreed. "It's just that I'll be laid up for quite a while yet." He frowned down at his bandaged arm.

Andrea leaned forward to set her dishes on the tray and felt something bump against her chest. Her hand reached up to touch it – the necklace that Al had given her! Almost without conscious thought, Andrea undid the clasp at her neck and put the necklace carefully on the tray in front of her. "I don't know what this is worth, Vance but I'd bet it's a lot. You can have it."

Vance's eyes nearly popped out of his head. "It looks like it's worth a fortune! You can't just go giving something like that away – where did you get it?" he asked suspiciously.

Andrea felt herself blush. "You know where it came from," she said shortly, "and I don't want it!" She leaned over and tapped the necklace with one finger. "It's yours, Vance. Use it to help get you out of those tunnels." When Vance made sounds of protest, Andrea merely spoke more loudly, drowning him out.

"I don't want it. I don't ever want to see it again. I feel like I was bought with it, like I sold myself out, myself and you. You taught me a lot about being a good friend, Vance. You taught me about loyalty and sticking by someone. Thank you for that."

"B-b-but," Vance sputtered, shaking his head. "You can't just go giving something like that away, Andy! Even if we are friends."

"Yes, I can," Andrea said firmly. Forgetting that she was supposed to be a boy, Andrea stood up and walked over to where Vance lay. She bent and kissed his flushed cheek.

Vance reacted with a jerk, balling his good hand into a fist. "That's the second or third time you've acted silly, lovey-dovey like that! It's almost like-like –" He stopped short, taking a good long look at the person standing before him. "Why, ya are a girl at that! Well, I'll be cow-kicked," he said in wonder. "Ya sure had me fooled! Now why would ya want ta be runnin' around in them tunnels like that? That's man's work!" He spoke indignantly. "Ya coulda got hurt!"

Andrea noticed with a smile that he had slipped

back into the gangster speech again. She was glad that her secret was finally out of the bag. "Yes, I could have gotten hurt, but at least I was there to save your skin! I rescued you, remember? Don't be such a male chauvinist."

"A what?" Looking puzzled, Vance scratched his head with his good hand.

"Never mind," Andrea sighed. "You wouldn't understand."

"Well, thank you for getting me out of the tunnels. If it wasn't for you, comin' after me, I don't know what would've happened."

The sun had sunk lower in the sky, indicating that evening would soon follow. There was something Andrea was supposed to do, but she couldn't quite remember what it was. "Well, you'll be able to take time to heal now without worrying about money," Andrea said, looking at the necklace. "And you can stay away from those tunnels and Big Al." She was smiling at Vance when she suddenly remembered.

"Big Al!" Andrea jumped out of the chair. "I'm supposed to meet him at seven o'clock at The Four Star Café! He warned me not to be late! Said he'd come looking for me…but he probably got caught in the raid."

"I wouldn't count on it," Vance stated flatly. "He's a weasel, never seems to get caught. Maybe you better go check it out, just in case."

"What time is it?!"

The grandfather clock in the hall chimed. It was fifteen minutes to the hour. "I have fifteen minutes to get there! Will I make it?"

"Sure," Vance told her. "But he's probably gonna guess that you're a girl, ya know. Ya never did look boyish enough."

"He already knows!" Andrea laughed. "He was the first to figure it out."

Vance shook his head. "I guess I was really blind! I just thought ya were a sickly lookin' boy! And what kind a girl has hair like that?!"

"Thanks a lot!" Andrea pushed his good arm lightly. "This hairstyle happens to be the fad right now, at least it is where I come from."

"Fad?" Vance questioned. "What's a fad? And where do you live?"

"Oh, never mind," Andrea sighed. "I don't have time to explain it all right now. Get Beanie to fill you in. She knows all my secrets." Andrea smiled, "But you probably won't believe her."

Vance had other things on his mind. "Ya really don't need to go back to the tunnels," he muttered. He seemed to be more concerned for her safety now that he knew she was a girl. "Just disappear. He won't come lookin' too hard for ya."

"I'd like to do that, but I need to check it out. I don't want him coming here to look for me. I don't want to put your family in any more danger."

"Well, if you think ya really need to…."

"Yeah," Andrea patted his shoulder. "I really need to, and I'd better go! I always seem to be in a rush around here. Do people ever slow down?"

"Don't forget the cap!" Vance yelled. "Ya don't want the whole world to know you're a girl!"

"Right! Thanks, Vance! And thank your mother for dinner. I'll be back here soon. I'll just go see what's happening in the tunnels." Andrea was quiet for a moment, thinking. "I guess I'll need to stay here for a while, Vance. But I'll pay my way, don't worry about that."

"With everything you've already done for us," Vance said, looking at the expensive necklace lying where Andrea had left it, "you can stay here for life!"

"Thanks, Vance," Andrea spoke quietly. I may need to, she thought sadly. "I gotta go now," Andrea said, as she turned and sprinted through the screen door and down the hall to Vance's room. She found the dusty and dirty blue cap on the dresser beside the water basin and realized that she hadn't made her bed. She turned to hastily throw the blankets across the mattress in some semblance of order. She didn't want Mrs. Talbot to think that she was a total slob. This done, she slammed the cap on her head and hastily tucked her short hair underneath. She was ready to go back into the tunnels to see if she could find out any news about Ol' Scarface.

Coming back to the porch, Andrea asked, "Where's the best place to get into the tunnels from here, Vance?"

"I'd go to the train station and enter through that janitor's room. It'll be crowded tonight with people coming and going. It should be easy for you to get in there unnoticed."

"Okay, then. See you later!" Andrea waved her hand as she ran lightly down the steps, across the street, and into the park. It was deserted now. Most people would be home having supper, she guessed.

It didn't take her long to jog the few blocks to the train station. It was very busy, as Vance had predicted. Andrea joined a group of people entering the station and let the flow carry her into the massive building. She walked across the marble floor and pulled open the heavy glass and wooden frame door that led down the stairs and out onto the tracks.

Andrea saw the policeman before he saw her. He was standing just inside the other doors, watching the people as they passed. He was looking for someone. He would surely see her if she disappeared into the caretaker's room and didn't emerge. Andrea stood for a moment letting people flow around her like water around a boulder in the stream. She didn't know what to do. How could she get into that room without causing any undue attention?

Leaning against the wall nearby was a large broom,

the kind the caretakers used at her school to sweep the floors. She picked up the broom and carried it slowly down the stairs hoping she looked like a caretaker.

The police officer didn't give her a second glance as she made her way over to the room. When he was looking the other way, she quickly opened the door and slipped inside. She was sure he would never think of her again. After all, she was just the janitor, doing her job.

Andrea quickly parked the broom against a wall and waited for her eyes to adjust to the darkness. She would never get used to that. It always frightened her a bit, to stand totally in the dark, unable to see. She knew that she would have to hurry.

If Big Al had not been caught, he would not like to be kept waiting. Andrea hoped that her little ploy with the empty cases and bottles had done the trick. She hoped that they had caught Old Scarface red-handed! He deserved to be in jail.

When Andrea was sure she could see at least a little bit, she crept over to the secret door and pushed her way through. As Andrea ran by the first lantern on the way to The Four Star Café, a hand suddenly snaked out, grabbing at her.

"Hey kid!" a voice boomed. Andrea was so startled that she hesitated a moment too long. The serpent arm whipped by and latched on to her shoulder. "Gotcha!" The force knocked Andrea clean off her feet and she fell to the floor with a thud. "Ya left us stranded!" the voice accused. "We're gonna get ya fer that!"

The men closed in on her, vengeance in their eyes. It was Chubs and Stilts! Apparently they had been unsuccessful in getting to the Imperial Hotel by tunnel last night, otherwise they would be calm and relaxed by now, having enjoyed their Turkish baths and illegal beverages. Andrea was petrified. Instinct took over. Adrenalin began to pump once more. What would Vance do in a situation like this? An idea popped into Andrea's mind.

Of course! She smiled and then looked down the tunnel. "Cops!" she yelled, pointing and waving wildly. "It's a raid!" The two men gasped and turned, scanning the dark tunnel for the authorities.

That was all the time Andrea needed. She was on her feet within seconds, careening down the tunnel at breakneck speed, escaping from the evil looking men.

Andrea's thoughts were churning a million miles a second. She wasn't watching where she was going as she neared The Four Star Café. She crashed headfirst into the pole and crumpled to the floor, knocking herself out for the second time in twenty-four hours....

7:05 PM Saturday Evening

TUNNELS OF TIME

A ndrea felt cold. She moaned and tried to move her head. It was stuck; she couldn't budge it. It was as if her noggin was being held in a giant vise grip. She raised her hand instead, to try to brush the icy cold feeling from her forehead. Something grasped her forearm and forced it down at her side again. Her fingers grasped short fibers, warm and cushioned: a soft, thick carpet.

Voices filled the air, murmuring and talking softly. Several persistently called her name, as if trying to awaken her from a deep, deep sleep. Andrea tried to answer, but her lips were glued together; her tongue, thick and woolly, had stapled itself to the roof of her mouth.

Her body felt amazingly calm and at rest, as if she floated in a pool of warm relaxing water. Andrea let the feeling wash over her in tiny riplets and tried to sink back into oblivion again, but a tiny thought kept niggling at her brain, refusing to let her body unwind totally. What was it? What was she trying to remember?

A deep male voice spoke loudly above her pounding head, causing her to moan softly. A fuzzy image forced its way inside her paralyzed brain, just beyond the realm of conscious thought. An unfocused picture of two men chasing her in a dark frightening place caused Andrea's prone body to stiffen with alarm. Two men! Running! Danger! She yelled and pushed herself violently upright into a sitting position. She had to get away! The men would hurt her!

Andrea thrashed her arms wildly about her, twisting and turning this way and that to try to free herself. "Let go! Let go! Leave me alone!" she yelled at the top of her voice.

"Andrea! Calm down!" Several people tried to soothe her.

"She's hysterical," another pronounced.

"Andrea!" A soft, quavering voice sounded in her ears.

"Grandma." Andrea turned toward the gentle sound and opened her eyes.

"She's awake!" Tony exclaimed. He tried to throw

himself onto Andrea in a child-like hug of gladness.

Andrea suddenly realized that she was sitting on the thick grey carpet of the restaurant, surrounded by her entire family. She was back in the present!

Everyone was talking at once. The sound waves caused her aching head to throb even more. Andrea rubbed her forehead, feeling the beginnings of a huge goose bump.

"…knocked yourself out, sweetheart," her father was explaining, "when you ran so hard into the mirror in the tunnel."

"Yeah!" Tony piped up. "I'm surprised you didn't break it! You should have heard the sound – Bang!"

Andrea surveyed her surroundings. She was definitely back to the wonderful, fabulous present! The dark, damp tunnels and cold, wet floors of packed earth and gravel had disappeared. Gone was the round wooden table that had stood in the centre of the large room. Once again Andrea saw the long banquet table, set for dinner, laden with glasses, cutlery, baskets of buns, and flickering candles. She glanced at the ceiling to find fluorescent lights shining down, bright and luminous.

Her wonderful family stood around her. Some knelt on the carpet nearby, anxious looks creasing their features. There was her father, sweetly holding her hand, and her mother, helping Grandmother to keep her calm. There was Tony, trying to look brave and confident, but he kept sneaking little peeks of anxiety her way. And Grandfather, standing back, surveying the whole scene, a tense look on his face. Andrea realized suddenly how much she loved them all, and how very much she had missed them during her absence, even pesky Cousin Richard and Vanessa.

Andrea grabbed Grandmother first and hugged her close. "You're the best, Grandmother!" She kissed her wrinkled cheek. "I missed you!"

"You missed me," Grandma twittered. "But I've been right here all along!"

"And Mom," Andrea wrapped her arms around her mother's shoulders, resting her head against her mother's chest. "I love you, Mom. You're the best mother in the whole world, even though we don't always agree on everything!"

Andrea's mother smiled and blinked back tears. "Why, thank you, Andrea." She brushed Andrea's hair back from her forehead and gently kissed her. "That's the nicest thing you've said to me in a long, long time."

Andrea grabbed her father's hand, as he stood looking down at her. "Sorry I was such a brat today, Dad, and wore the wrong clothes. I didn't mean to embarrass you. I did know what to wear, I was just being obstinate and pig-headed. You're neat for a father, kind and consistent. I'm glad you're my dad!" Andrea said, thinking of Ol' Scarface.

Mr. Talbot smiled down at his daughter and then gathered her close for a brief hug. "So I'm consistent, eh?" He gave Andrea a puzzled look. "What a funny thing to say, but I accept your apology. I can see that you're maturing as we speak, my dear. You're growing up!"

If only he knew, Andrea thought, thinking back to the tunnels. She glanced toward Tony. She wanted to give him a hug to let him know that she loved him, even though they teased one another and got on each other's nerves sometimes. He hovered just out of reach, a silly smile on his face, looking as if he could read her mind. She smiled at him and he took a step closer. It was all the space Andrea needed. She grabbed him in a bear hug and kissed his chubby cheek.

"You're a great brother, Tony. I'm glad that we're friends," she whispered as he squirmed out of her grasp.

"Yuck, girl germs," Tony mocked, making a big show of wiping the kiss from his face. Andrea smiled, wanting to laugh out loud, to spin and shout. If her head hadn't been throbbing so painfully, she would have. She was back! Back to the present! Living in her own time and with a kid brother who teased her and whom she loved to tease. And in time for Vanessa's wedding!

By the look of things, she had only been knocked out for a few minutes. Had she just dreamed all the adventures in the underground tunnels!? It didn't seem possible; everything had seemed so real. And yet, how could it have been?

"Here's another ice pack." A strange voice spoke from above. Andrea had to crane her neck to look that far up. The voice sounded vaguely familiar. She tried to identify it. A man stood almost directly above her, his features silhouetted against the bright lights shining from the ceiling.

Mrs. Talbot took the ice pack and gently placed it on her daughter's forehead. "That's going to be some bump tomorrow."

"Just in time for wedding pictures!" Cousin Richard sneered. "That's going to look just great! A junior bridesmaid with a lump the size of an ostrich egg on her forehead!"

"Richard!" Grandma admonished. "It's not really Andrea's fault that she ran into the looking glass."

"Then whose fault is it?" Tony asked simply.

"Of course it's my fault," Andrea replied quietly. "I should have paid more attention and not been so silly."

Everyone fell silent in surprise. This was not the Andrea they knew. "I think we'd better take her to the hospital," Richard wryly suggested. "That doesn't sound like Andrea at all." Everyone laughed, relieved that Andrea was all right. It made a merry sound that bounced off the walls.

Andrea glanced at her Grandfather, hovering in the

background and smiling at her from across the room. He looked as if he wanted to rush over and engulf her in his arms, but something held him back. Aunt Bea stood beside him, fluttering this way and that, excited and trembling fingers pressed against her lips. They looked different somehow, but Andrea couldn't put her finger on what it was.

"How do you feel, Andrea?" Her father asked, breaking into her jumbled thoughts. He felt her pale, dry cheek with the back of his hand.

"A little dizzy and I have a headache," Andrea reported, turning her attention to her father. "Besides that, I think I'm all right." She struggled to her feet as several pairs of eager hands helped steady her. She took a small step.

"Sit down here." That same strangely familiar male voice spoke at Andrea's side. She gratefully slid into the soft chair indicated, as she glanced up at the speaker.

"B-Big Al?" she stuttered, drawing back, fear written all over her face. Her first instinct was to run away as fast as possible. Instead, she stared directly at the man, squinting thoughtfully. Big Al, and yet this man was so much older, with his wizened, pale skin and thinning hair. He was Big Al and yet he wasn't! How could it be?!

"Big Al?!" Richard repeated looking from Andrea to the man and back again.

"Who is 'Big Al'?"

Andrea continued to stare at the man: he was the right height, but the scar was somehow different, not quite as vivid as Big Al's had been. It looked more like a wrinkle.

The man laughed, his face creasing in surprise. "My name is Al, all right – Alan Saunders." He shook his head in amusement. "I own this place, remember? It's been the family business for a couple of generations, since the 1920s.

"But no one has ever called me 'Big Al,' except...." he paused for a moment, a soft look of remembering suddenly crossing his lined face. "Except my mother. She sometimes confuses me with my father, especially now that she's getting older...."

This was Big Al's son! It had to be, Andrea thought. And in that case his mother was probably..."Rosie!" Andrea exclaimed. Was it possible?

Alan Saunders's head jerked up at the mention of the name. "How do you know?" he breathed, staring at Andrea as if she had suddenly grown three heads!

"Rosie's your mother," Andrea repeated firmly. There was no doubt in her mind. It had to be true.

Alan hesitated, then nodded, smoothing his thinning hair across a bald spot on his head. "But nobody ever called her that, except...."

"Your father...." Andrea finished for him. "Big Al."

"My mother never told me a thing about my father,

except his name. He was out of the picture before I was even born. It's all such a mystery!" Alan laughed, uncomfortable that all of the attention was suddenly focused on him. "This is too bizarre, you've hit your head too hard. I think we'd better get you to the doctor. You've got a concussion."

Andrea let the matter drop. Now was not the time to have a heart-to-heart discussion with the man. Besides, he wouldn't want to hear it from her – a kid and a perfect stranger. She wondered why Rosie had never shared her story with her son.

After all, he deserved to know the truth about his father. Maybe she had found it much too painful to talk about. Maybe she still despised Ol' Scarface for what he had done. This was proof, then, Andrea realized! She must have gone back in time. There was no other explanation for the fact that she had met and shared adventures with Big Al and Rosie, and now their son stood before her, an almost identical version of Old Scarface, but much older.

"I don't need to go to the doctor," Andrea declared. "I just need to eat and sit down for a while."

"Well," her mother said, uncertainly, "if you think so, Andrea. But if you start to feel sick, in any way, I want to know."

Andrea nodded meekly. "Yes, Mother," she said in a slightly mocking tone.

"Now that's the Andrea I know and love!" her father

exclaimed, patting her shoulder. "We have our own dear Andrea back."

Everyone laughed and resumed their places around the table. The talking and laughter flowed again, everyone relieved that Andrea had not been hurt too badly. A young waitress came clattering down the stairs. "Dinner will be served in approximately five minutes," she informed the guests.

Five minutes. That gave Andrea time to go and freshen up. She needed time alone, time to ponder all of the thoughts jumbling her brain. She leaned over and whispered in her grandmother's ear. "Where's the ladies' room?"

"I'll show her the way," Aunt Bea said. Andrea sighed impatiently, looking down the table at old Aunt Bea. All she needed was to put up with her antics right now. But it would be rude to refuse, and Andrea was learning that everyone deserved respect. She nodded in acquiescence, and Bea pushed her chair back, grinning brightly at Andrea.

Andrea studied the lively blue eyes, wondering where she had seen them before. Aunt Bea was acting even weirder than usual, Andrea thought, as she followed her up the stairs.

"There's someone here who would like to see you," Bea smiled as they reached the top step and turned right toward the washrooms. Her blue eyes twinkled merrily, making her look years younger.

Who would want to meet me, Andrea thought wryly, unless it was one of Bea's equally eccentric friends. Oh well, Andrea supposed she could put up with that for a minute or two. She glanced around the restaurant. Must be a popular place, she thought, judging by the hordes of people laughing and waiting to be served. The old-fashioned, high wooden benches and booths were filled to capacity.

Andrea stood for a moment from her vantage point in the rear of the restaurant watching the scene before her. Alan Saunders has a great business going here, she thought. She wondered if Big Al had been the restaurant's first owner back in the early days.

"Hello, Andrea," a quavery voice greeted her.

Andrea whirled to find a very old woman sitting in a wheelchair. Her skin was clear and delicately drawn over fine bones. Even with wrinkles and white shimmering hair, Andrea knew who it was.

"Rosie!" Impulsively Andrea bent and gently pressed her cheek against Rosie's.

"He never came back, you know." The old woman stated without emotion. "Not that I would have wanted him, but it would have been nice to let him know he had a son. I tried to keep track of him through the newspapers, but in those days news didn't travel as far – not like it does today."

"He would be very proud of his son," Andrea assured her. "He seems like a nice man. He looks like

Ol' Scarface, but thank goodness he doesn't act like him. But what about the scar?" Andrea wanted to know. "How did that happen?"

"I don't know how it happened. I guess my whole being was centred on Big Al all during my pregnancy. I thought of him constantly, angry at him for dumping me in that way, and yet I was glad to be having a baby, even though in my time it was very taboo for a woman to have a child out of wedlock. When Alan was born, he had that imprint on his cheek – like a brand. It was all so extraordinary. But then, that time spent with you was pretty fantastic too. I always knew there was something different about you. You just didn't seem to fit into my world."

Andrea smiled. "No, I didn't, and now you know why."

The old woman grasped Andrea's arm. "I sure do!" She laughed, a lusty Rosie laugh that seemed funny coming from such a frail old lady. "I feel strange trying to fit into this modern world now. I can't use a cell phone. I have trouble with a microwave, and I'm not sure what a discman is. Talk about changes! I feel like I'm the time traveller now. Truth to tell, I miss the old times."

Andrea laughed and bent to kiss Rosie's soft cheek again. She sure was kissing a lot of strangers these days – and yet it seemed right somehow. After all, she had shared dangerous adventures with these people. It was only right that they should have feelings for each other. "Whatever happened to Beanie and Vance?" Andrea asked sadly. "I'm going to miss them. I never even got to say goodbye. They won't know what happened to me."

Rosie choked delicately, staring up at Bea. "Didn't you tell her yet?!"

Bea smiled, taking Andrea's arm. "Not yet, but we have five minutes before dinner is served. Do you think that's long enough to catch up on so many years of news?"

THE REST OF THE EVENING PASSED in a blur. Andrea's mind was still in the tunnels, trying to understand what had happened. It was simple, really. She had gone back in time and spent an evening with Vance, Big Al, and Rosie, dodging the police and having the adventure of a lifetime.

But Andrea knew that she could not say that to her parents. No one would believe her. It sounded impossible, and yet it had happened. Andrea had proof. She had Alan Saunders, with his scarred face, old Rosie, who remembered her from years before, and most importantly, she suddenly realized, she still had Vance's cap!

Grandpa Talbot had picked it up off the carpet during all the confusion and had been holding on to it ever since. When Aunt Bea and Andrea had finally rejoined the group, he hurried over. "Thanks for bringing it back to me, Andrea," he said, holding it gently in his large hands. "It's been gone for so long. Imagine that! It looks a little worse for wear. It sure went through some tough times with you that night."

Andrea ran her forefinger along the tattered brim. "But h-how did it come back with me?!" It didn't seem possible, but there it was, dirty, dusty and smelling faintly of stale tunnel air.

"I have some things to show you, Andrea Talbot, that didn't come back with you. And I'll bet you'll be amazed to see them! I've been saving these, like I promised I would, wondering if I'd ever get the chance to return them to you."

Aunt Bea opened her large purse and pulled out a small jewellery box. She opened it tenderly. There, nestled in the soft cotton batting were two very decrepit looking barrettes. They once had been shiny white, but were now yellowed with age and very brittle. They should have spelled 'A-N-D-R-E-A' and 'T-A-L-B-O-T,' but several letters were missing. "I kept them forever, just like I said I would." Aunt Bea beamed at Andrea, looking more like Beanie the child than an elderly lady.

"Bea wore them constantly," Grandpa Talbot – Vance – remembered. "She was never without them. Did you know that she even changed her name? She became Beatrice Andrea Talbot. Since she hadn't been given a middle name, she adopted 'Andrea' as her second name. And she talked about you all the time! It was Andrea Talbot this, and Andrea Talbot that! Now you know why she always calls you 'Andrea Talbot'."

Andrea grinned at her great aunt and impulsively threw her arms around the old lady. "I don't think I'll be able to call you 'Aunt Bea' again! You'll always be good old 'Beanie' to me! You were right, Beanie! We did find each other! And we do have a lot in common!"

Andrea smiled as she listened to Beanie and Grandpa Talbot chat back and forth. They were so excited! It was almost as if her time-travelling adventure had made them younger. Or perhaps it was that Andrea now saw them in a much different light. They weren't just old Grandpa Talbot and eccentric, elderly Aunt Bea. They were her good friends, Vance and Beanie, the young people she had shared adventures and danger with. Now when Andrea looked at them she didn't even see wrinkling skin and white hair. She saw Vance, with his quick, lop-sided smile, and bright-eyed Beanie. Andrea hoped that she would always see them in this way.

She thought about her time in yesterday Moose Jaw. There were still a few things she needed to know. Andrea waited until the conversation between Beanie and Vance slowed down and then she asked, "Whatever happened to Big Al? Did he get caught that night? Did anyone ever take over his territory? And what about that big meeting? What was that all about?"

"Ahhh!" Beanie laughed gleefully. "I knew you'd

want to know about all that, but let's handle one question at a time." She dug around in her large bag and came up with an ancient-looking envelope which she handed to Andrea. "Here, I saved this just for you. Go ahead. Look inside."

Andrea carefully opened the tattered envelope and pulled out a small yellowed piece of paper. It was a newspaper clipping many decades old. It practically crumbled in Andrea's trembling fingers. She held it very gently as she scanned the article. "Raid on Moose Jaw Residence," the headline screamed in big bold letters. The article went on to describe a raid that had been made on a Moose Jaw home in the early hours of Saturday morning after liquor bottles and cases were found strewn on the porch and in the nearby street. The names of those arrested were listed.

"But Big Al's name isn't here." Andrea was surprised.

"No," Beanie answered. "He wasn't found that morning. Actually, he was never seen again in Moose Jaw."

"And the meeting," Andrea asked again. "What was that all about?"

"I never did find out. It could have all been a hoax to divert attention from something else going on in town. It could have been Ol' Scarface's way of finding out who his faithful people were. Those gangsters often tested their people in funny ways. That Al

Capone was slippery as an otter," Grandpa Talbot stated. "And he wasn't always telling the truth when he talked to a person. You were wise to take everything he said with a grain of salt. I guess I finally learned that lesson the hard way," he chuckled, shaking his head. "There were various rumours about Al Capone being in town later on, but it was never confirmed."

"You mean, Big Al was actually –" Andrea gasped.

"Al Capone!" Beanie and Grandpa Talbot loudly declared.

"Wow! A famous gangster! And to think I actually met him!" Then Andrea thought about what could have happened. "Gee, we were all so lucky! We could have really been in danger!"

"We were in real danger, Andrea," Grandpa Talbot reminded her. "There's no telling what could have happened to us, and I sure took a beating." He smiled gratefully at Andrea and pulled her into his arms. "But you saved me. You were very brave, my dear. I'm very proud of you. When the chips were down and we needed help and a friend, you were there for us. Even though you were afraid of the dangers and worried about getting back to the future, you put our needs first."

Beanie nodded. "You sure did."

"But maybe we scared Ol' Scarface off, Andrea, with our little stunt of spreading the bottles all over the steps!" Beanie changed the subject.

"Maybe," Andrea agreed. She shivered just thinking

about the danger. "Those must have been very tough years back then."

Grandpa nodded. "They were. Money was scarce, especially for families like ours – a single-parent family with no father to bring in the money. That beautiful necklace of yours sure came in handy, Andrea. Mother sold it and got enough money to pay out the mortgage on the boarding house! There was some left over to make a few renovations. After that wonderful piece of good fortune we were much better off." Grandpa smiled at Andrea, his blue eyes shining, and Andrea felt warmed by his love.

She was so-o-o-o glad to be back! She wanted to run around to every person in the room and give them each a huge bear hug! Instead, she smiled at Beanie, who winked and grinned back. Andrea knew that she would think often in the days and weeks to come of her fantastic adventure. She and Aunt Bea and Grandpa Talbot had a lot of talking to do. It still didn't seem possible, and yet it had happened. No wonder Great Aunt Beanie and Grandpa Talbot were so fond of her! And she was very fond of them. They had shared special times and wonderful adventures, not to mention breath-stealing, spine-tingling dangers. She couldn't wait to talk and talk with them! It would be fun, just like the times they had spent so many years ago! But first, they had a rehearsal and a wedding to get through....

TUNNEL, WHAT TUNNEL?

The wedding rehearsal went the way of all rehearsals. The wedding party was giddy and foolish, wasting time being silly. The young minister smiled at it all, letting the party get rid of its nervous tension. He seemed to have endless patience and a smile for everyone.

"The wedding will go without a hitch tomorrow," he assured the worried bride and groom when the attendants had tripped chaotically down the aisle, arriving in a bunch, forgetting to take the bridesmaids' arms. "That seems to be the way it works. Having an awkward, rough rehearsal makes for a beautiful, well-staged wedding." Encouraged, the bridal party went through the ceremony one more time before calling it a night. Andrea wasn't the least bit nervous now. After the adventures and life-threatening situations she had faced in the tunnels, the simple and safe role of junior bridesmaid didn't even faze her.

Soon everyone split up and left the church to go and get some rest before the big event. Andrea's family was staying at Grandpa and Grandma Talbot's house, a big old rambling place with many bedrooms and a huge airy basement. That's where Andrea and Vanessa would be spending the night, in a large room in the basement called The Office.

It was tradition in the Talbot family. The brides had to spend the night at the grandparents' house. No one seemed to know where the tradition had come from, but it was followed as religiously as the ceremony would be the next day.

Andrea had been none too happy to learn that she would be sharing her basement bedroom with Vanessa, the nervous bride. But that was before her escapade in the tunnels. Now it didn't matter to her at all. She only wanted a nice clean comfortable bed in which to lay her weary body. Once her head hit the pillow, Andrea was sure that she would sleep.

Neat twin beds greeted the girls as they entered the large room. It had rather large windows for a basement, allowing the light to filter in during the daytime. The closet stood open, awaiting their clothes, but Andrea didn't bother to unpack. She merely hung her wedding clothes in the closet and shut the door. "You can use the bathroom first," she offered Vanessa.

"Thanks." Vanessa stared at her younger cousin for a moment, then smiled. "You usually don't think of others first," she commented quietly. "I guess you are growing up."

Andrea flopped down on her bed, turning her nose into the bedspread to smell the clean fresh fragrance. It was wonderful to be back in the present! She smiled at the light switch on the wall and the tri-light lamp in the corner. She smiled at the computer sitting on the desk under the window. Grandpa used it to keep track of his business accounts. He was such a computer whiz. Grandma used it to keep track of her recipes and to write letters to friends and family. The grandchildren mainly used it to play games. Andrea even smiled at the old wardrobe in the corner of the room. It had been there since the house had been built – old and dear and very familiar.

It was great to be back to a familiar, safe place. Andrea lay on the bed feeling completely relaxed for the first time in over twenty-four hours. She fell into an exhausted lethargy, thoughts of her night's adventures still playing in her mind like reruns of a wonderful and exciting movie. Actually, it all seemed more like a movie than real life!

Vanessa returned a full thirty minutes later, freshly

showered, the radiant look still shimmering on her clean features. "You look so happy," Andrea exclaimed.

"Thanks, Andy," Vanessa said, dropping on the bed to give Andrea an impulsive hug. "And I really am glad that you're going to be my junior bridesmaid. I know you feel frightened by the role...."

"Not any more," Andrea admitted. After her tunnel adventure, she doubted the she would ever be afraid to tackle anything again. "Actually, I'm kind of glad to be part of the wedding party. I've never had the chance before now, and I do feel honoured that you wanted me to be a part of it, especially after some of the nasty stunts I pulled when I was younger."

"Like cutting my hair?" Vanessa grinned at Andrea's embarrassed expression.

Andrea nodded. "Yes. I was very jealous of you and your perfect manners, your beautiful hair, and your blue Talbot eyes. I've always wanted the Talbot eyes."

Vanessa had grabbed a brush and was busy pulling it through her wet hair. "Bet you didn't know that I was envious of your easy charm and athletic body. You could do so many things that I couldn't do, things that I was afraid to do."

Andrea smiled over at Vanessa, surprise written all over her face. "What?! You were envious of me!?" Vanessa nodded, a smile touching her lips. "You know," Andrea said after a few moments, "I'm glad you're my cousin. I can't imagine having to grow up without you there." She reached over to give Vanessa a hug.

"You are changing, Cousin. You're growing up. Maybe now, you and I can be more friends than enemies. What do you think? And guess what, I love your beautiful brown eyes!"

Andrea smiled sheepishly. "Thanks. I'm beginning to like them too. I guess it's good to be different in some ways. Talbot blue is great, but very common in this family. Chocolate brown is unique and that makes it special!" They laughed, blue eyes shining into brown.

"And yes," Andrea continued, "I'm sure we can be friends. It would be nice to be able to share things with you." They hugged again, then Andrea remembered how dusty and sweaty she was. The quick wash in the basin at Vance's house had helped some, but it was nothing compared to modern bathing methods.

"Let me at that shower!" Andrea exclaimed, breaking the mood. She was sure looking forward to hot steamy water with lots of soap and shampoo! She jumped up and quickly stripped off her stained, grimy overalls, standing in her huge ancient T-shirt, which could have easily passed for a short mini-dress. Bunching the overalls up, Andrea flung them into a corner of the room. A soft jangle sounded as the overalls hit the wall. Something started to roll across the tiled floor, echoing eerily in the sudden stillness of the night.

"What's that noise?" Vanessa asked lazily from the bed. She sat up straighter to watch the progression of the object. It rolled across the room and under the old wooden cupboard where it bumped into something with a quiet thump, fell over, and was silent.

Andrea shrugged unconcerned. "It's probably just a penny." She had forgotten all about the last coin Big Al had tossed at her a lifetime ago. She began to gather her toiletries from her bag on the floor in preparation for her shower.

"Aren't you going to get it?" Vanessa asked.

"I'll get it later," Andrea replied, shrugging her shoulders. "It's no big deal, and besides, it's not going anywhere."

"Come on," Vanessa hopped off the bed. "I'll help you move this cupboard, so you can reach it better."

"It's not that important, Vanessa. Really. Don't worry about it."

"It's probably a tooney," Vanessa said, using the nickname for the two-dollar coin. She gave the cupboard a push, but it didn't budge. "Give me a hand, Andy, it's your money." When it came to money, anyone's money, Vanessa was very prudent. She was one who would put chewing gum on the end of a stick to get money out of the sewer drain. She would stand in the middle of Main Street, Moose Jaw, cars bearing down, to pick up a penny. Andrea knew that Vanessa would never rest until the coin was rescued from under the wooden cupboard.

"Oh, all right," Andrea sighed, putting her bath supplies down on the bed. "On the count of three," she said as she put her hands on the wooden cupboard. A strange feeling of déjà vu hit her and she shook her head to clear it. She could have been back down in the basement of Rosie's apartment helping Beanie come up with a plan! "One, two, three." Both girls pushed and heaved. The old wooden cupboard didn't even budge.

"It's heavier than I thought," Vanessa grunted. "But I'm sure we can get it to move. Let's try again." Both girls gave an extra hard push and the wooden dresser slid a few centimetres. "Push, Andrea!" Vanessa ordered.

"I am pushing," Andrea replied, her voice distorted from the effort. They both pushed, groaning from the weight of the heavy wooden cupboard.

Suddenly it moved, swinging open, as if on a hinge, revealing the coin on the floor. "Here's your money, Andy," Vanessa said bending to pick up the offending piece. She studied it carefully turning it over in her palm. "It's not a tooney." With the coin safely in her hand, Vanessa stood, head bent, examining it.

"This is very unusual and old-looking, Andy. Where did you get it?" When Andrea didn't reply, Vanessa glanced back at her. "Andy?!"

Andrea was frozen to the spot, her face ghostly pale, her mouth hanging open in shock and disbelief. Vanessa turned around to stare straight ahead at what should have been the wall. But the wall was gone. Instead, a black gaping hole beckoned her into the darkness....

ACKNOWLEDGEMENTS

Thanks to Claire Brown and her students at Brevoort Park School, Saskatoon, 1997-98, for suggesting the title. And to Nicole Chauvin-King and her class at École Victoria School, Saskatoon, 1997-98, for their encouragement and suggestions.

ABOUT THE AUTHOR

MARY HARELKIN BISHOP is a teacher-librarian in the Saskatoon Public School system. In addition to her fiction writing for children, Mary has published poetry and short fiction, in the Courtney Milne book *Prairie Dreams* and in "Green's Magazine." *Tunnels of Time* is her first book publication.

Born in Michigan, Mary arrived in Saskatoon in 1970. She lives there with her husband and two teenaged children.